PRAISE FOR TIM McGUIRE AND THE RAINMAKER:

"Tim McGuire writes a good Western, the story fast-paced, the characters vividly drawn."

—Larry McMurtry

"No writer working handles the traditional Western better than Tim McGuire. His lean, muscular style and assured knowledge of the frontier should guarantee him a place on the shelves beside Louis L'Amour and Jack Schaefer."

—Loren D. Estleman

"Fast and action-packed. Tim McGuire has given us a terrific traditional Western novel with one of those rare, unforgettable characters."

—Robert J. Conley on *Nobility*

"A solid read with good characterization and a cliffhanger of an ending. Surely we can expect to see more of the Rainmaker."

—*Book News* on *Danger Ride*

"For those who like action in their Westerns, Tim McGuire [has] plenty of it, from start to finish."

—Elmer Kelton

THE EDGE OF THE BLADE

The Winchester flew from Cole's hands. The impact that took it came from the left. Cole glanced that way. Hard wood smashed against his jaw. He fell back. On the ground, he rammed his heel at the presence hovering above. A loud gasp meant he'd landed the kick. He scrambled to his feet. Rapid footsteps from behind turned him about. His first focus was a steel edge coming directly between his eyes.

He rammed his hand at the object. The wood handle slapped against his palm. He wrapped his thumb and fingers around it and pushed the ax away from his forehead, knocking his hat to the ground.

His jaw aching, he tried ripping the ax from the attacker, but a punch to his belly dropped him to the dirt. Through the haze he saw the blade being drawn overhead as if to split a log, only it was his head that was the target....

THE LAW OF THE BARBARY COAST

TIM McGUIRE

LEISURE BOOKS NEW YORK CITY

To those Americans in uniform, at
their posts here and overseas, past and present.
Thank you for your service, which allows me to do this.

A LEISURE BOOK®

July 2006

Published by

Dorchester Publishing Co., Inc.
200 Madison Avenue
New York, NY 10016

ISBN 0-8439-5228-8

Visit us on the web at www.dorchesterpub.com.

To the DFW Writers' Workshop
for not only their acceptance but their
promotion of my success as one of
their notable achievements.

The Extraordinary Adventures
and Exploits of the Legendary
Frontiersman and U.S. Marshal

THE RAINMAKER

Follow his chase on the trail of

COY DALLAS

the notorious bandit, outlaw

and murderer of the innocent

in

A HUNG JURY

as told by renowned

"Scribe of the West"

DICK "THE DANDY" JOHNSON

CHAPTER ONE

A lightning flash illuminated the night sky, sending rain down onto the Earth with the force of a waterfall. Through the storm's fury, a light shone in the dark like a beacon. The sharply inclined hills and muddy ground caused the palomino to miss many steps. It had been a long night. It had been a long trail.

He angled through the short thick brush, using the light as a guide. As rain pelted his shoulders and wide-brimmed hat, he finally pulled up to the front. He tethered the palomino to the post, where many other mounts stood waiting for their riders. A moment's pause gave thought that he'd only rest a short while, just long enough to ask a question.

Maybe he'd have some hot coffee to take the chill from his bones, he thought, then seek suitable shelter until the storm passed. He ducked beneath the short awning between the heavy streams of runoff, then shrugged the slicker from his shoulders and shook it free of drops. Before he took hold of the latch, he palmed the grip of the holstered Colt .45 in case the company inside weren't ready for strangers.

At first he pushed gently, not knowing how sturdy the aged wood was, but when it stuck against the water-swollen jamb, he shoved it open. The door swung wide and he stood in the threshold, a bit embarrassed for the attention-grabbing entrance.

All eyes came his way. He entered, not comfortable with turning his back to reach for the latch now so far away, so he hooked his heel to swing it shut while still eyeing the crowd stuck in the small structure. In little time, the folks resumed what was on their minds before, allowing him to go to the long narrow plank where a hefty barkeep stood in front of a shelf of bottles and jugs. Single-flame lanterns hung one apiece on the four walls, making it hard to see far, but he moved through the elbows and shoulders to stand in front of the center of the plank. A moment passed before the bartender came his way.

"Whiskey?"

A shake of the head was the answer, but a louder than normal answer was needed to cut through the reverie of the room. "Coffee." The order seemed to perplex the barkeep. A man lacking the want for spirits in the middle of a cold night wasn't common, but he'd stuck to coffee for many years. The hefty man went around the end of the plank to retrieve the pot that hung over the small fire pit at the back wall. Once back with it, he pulled a tin from the shelf and filled it. The steaming brew was inviting, but he hadn't come just for that. He put the coin on the plank as payment, then leaned forward to ask discreetly, "This California land?"

The question further perplexed the barkeep. "Where'd you think it was?"

The terse answer was expected and easily ignored. Before he singed his lips on the hot coffee, he needed to know one other answer. "How far to San Francisco?"

The answer didn't come immediately. The hefty man seemed more concerned to fill glasses and collect his take before giving away free advice. After all the patrons had been served, he looked back to reply. "Hundred and fifty miles, give or take."

The distance was both reward and disappointment. With his eyes fixed on the steaming coffee, the recollection of the trail to this spot came to mind. The decision to head West was made three months ago, north of Montana in the rocky hills of Canada, chasing after the killer Coy Dallas. While he had followed the markings of the bandits, ideas swirled about finding his true freedom—a freedom he hadn't known for nearly seven years. Ever since that cool summer morning on the Greasy Grass when he watched the slaughter of the Seventh, branded a traitor by the army for being missing during the charge, he ran, forever dogged by the mention of his own name among those looking for him.

The plan to face the charges against him took him to the only man he trusted not to put a bullet in his back. Once in Copper Springs, Montana, he received an unexpected welcome. The time in a cell waiting to travel to Helena brought the first small peace in some time. The townsfolk thought he was a hero, or perhaps a freak. In either case, he didn't mind the woman-cooked meals and the shelter of a roof. An evening with a red-haired foreign beauty further pushed him away from the plan. It was the most delight he had enjoyed since having a woman of his own ten years before. Or so he dreamed. He wanted to find out more about her. Then came the news that the man he trusted went missing while chasing Dallas.

The notion of pinning on a star wasn't an easy one, but necessary to ride in a land respectful of the law. The idea of nursemaiding a nosy reporter from the East wasn't his choice either, but was also needed in order to have the supplies for the manhunt.

The discovery of the blood left in the bandits' wake—and the shortening of those lives—brought more thought about his own. If he were ever to know pure, lasting peace, where he might come and go and do as he pleased, it wouldn't be at the hands of a military tribunal. With his short duty as a law-man done, he came west across the Great Divide and over the Bitterroots to a land he'd never seen, seeking one more glimpse of that red-haired beauty.

Loud shouts from behind shook him from his daze. He turned to spot two stocky men seated at a table halfway through a whiskey bottle, announcing to all what was on their minds, whether it was asked for or not. He ignored their yammerings about deeds done in the past and turned his attention back to the barkeep.

"Any towns between here and there?"

The hefty man shrugged. "Plenty of mining camps in these hills. Don't know if you'd call them towns. But there's men there." He refilled a few more glasses.

"Mining camps?" The familiarity of the practice meant another question needed asking. "You heard of a woman singer?" The barkeep's attention wasn't fully focused on answering. A few steps to the side, displacing a few patrons along the way, allowed him to face the hefty man squarely. "A foreigner woman. Tall lady, with red hair?" The barkeep dipped his eyes, a sign of consideration. Laughter drowned the next question, so it had to be asked again, only louder. "Her name is Vivien. Vivien Hooper." The inquiry brought more notice than desired, but if it meant a worthy reply, he'd ignore the interested ears.

The barkeep nodded. "I seen the name on some banners." The barkeep moved further toward the wall.

If there was more to learn, he'd have to move the same way as the hefty man. "Banners? Where?" To stay in front of the man meant plowing through those with elbows settled on the plank. A few took exception. Matching glares with those of shorter stature proved sufficient to get the path cleared in order to continue the questions. "Where'd you see these banners?"

A shake of the head held no promise. "Can't remember."

The hope of finding her didn't wash away so easy. Maybe there was another way around to the truth. "How far back did you see them?"

Another shrug accompanied a few more shakes of the head. "I don't know, mister. Why you want to know? She your wife?"

The suggestion instantly put a vision of her being so in his head. However, the truth quickly dissolved it. Yet, the wondering of what could be, especially after how vivid the experience was of her trapped in his brain, had him sidestep the true answer to seek another. "I just need to know if she passed by these parts, and maybe where she was headed.

She's a singer. Saw her last at a mining town in Montana, name of Copper Springs. I heard she was headed to Butte and a few other parts south and west. But she stays in San Francisco. She may make some stops on the way. You know, sing for some men in some camps."

More glasses needed filling, but at least it didn't deter a reply. "A bunch of shows come up and down these hills. Can't remember all of them."

The point was understandable, but the remembrance of her features, some parts clothed and some parts not, brought a smirk. "Oh, you'd take notice of this one. Tall, like I said. Skin almost as white as milk. Thin neck but a small nose. Talks with a cut to her words. She's from some place she calls As . . . Austere . . . Austermalian."

"Australia?"

He pointed at the familiar word. "That's it. You know her?"

"I heard of the place," was the gruff answer. "But I don't know her. Hell, there's Australians, Germans, Irish, and all sorts of people in this state. All came here for the gold back in forty-nine and haven't left. Just because a gal is from Australia doesn't mean I heard of her."

The lecture didn't sway him from seeking more information. "Yeah, I know all that." The barkeep moved further away, a motion to show he didn't want to answer any more questions. It was a move he often used himself. "But she doesn't live here. I mean not in California." A few more steps were needed to regain the hefty man's attention. "She's leaving back for that place soon and I'm trying to catch up with her."

A bump from the right came a split second before

a hand probed around his waist. He grabbed at the hand, but a weight was missing from his hip. Between the shoulders and heads, he snatched the thieving grip of a puny whisker-faced old-timer. Before he could find the missing item, he saw it tossed to one of the stocky braggarts at the table.

"Here you go, Will." The Colt .45 was caught in the air at the table by the one with half a scalp of hair. A smile showed a pair of gapped front teeth and not many more behind.

Blood pounded through the veins with the same fury as the storm outside. During the effort to gain information he'd let his caution lapse. The error cost him the means used to stay alive the last seven years. As the clamor of voices quickly subsided, the stocky man with a giddy laugh inspected the pistol.

"Nice piece." He looked down his nose. "Where'd you get it?"

With all eyes fixed on him, including the hefty bartender, he gauged the distance between himself and the pistol at little more than ten feet, with no less than a dozen bodies, two that were female, in the way. If he were to rush after it, he'd take at least one, maybe two, slugs before he got near. The better tactic was to play along. "Army issue."

A nod of respect was meant for the Colt. "What it looked like." Their eyes finally met. "It's why I asked. You a soldier?"

"Was." He scanned about the curious faces. None were familiar. "Once."

"Well, what are you doing here?"

Thunder outside reflected his mood. "Free country. What are you doing here?"

"Me?" He grinned and chuckled. "I'm Will Hayward. Been here nearly twenty-five years." He

propped the butt of the Colt against his woolen
vest, which covered another bright red one, all atop
a white-collared shirt. The cock of the hammer
cleared the dozen bodies with the two females in an
instant for a direct line of fire. "I was asking you."

An eye on the muzzle prepared him to see fire at
any instant. It was time for a deep breath to ease the
air. "See here, mister. I really don't want to tangle
with you. It's been a long day. If I done something
for you or your friends to take offense, I'll say now
I'm sorry for doing so. I'd be obliged for the return
of my weapon and I'll take my leave of this place
with no harm done."

The giddy laugh pierced the room. It was a signal
that he wasn't just talking to the man with the gun,
but also to the half bottle of whiskey gone.

"Sounds awful like a man with a yellow streak in
him. Especially strange for one carrying around a
big piece like this one."

"Just the same, I'm offering to leave."

"Why? So you can go out there and bring in another? Maybe a Sharps rifle? Spencer maybe?" The
one called Will shook his head. "Don't imagine that
being a good idea. Not for somebody been shamed
as you have." That grin shared the truth to all. It
would be a fool's move to let a shamed man out of
sight so he could get bigger firepower. Peeks to the
side made the room feel smaller than when he entered. The storm kept the folks inside as an excuse
to watch. If they had a cloudless night they'd have
stayed anyway. Although likely it wasn't the first
time at this bar, the spilling of blood still wasn't a
sight to miss.

A moment's notion to turn calmly for the door
would shift the shame to the shooter. A slug would

take him down before he gripped the latch. Either choice wouldn't be his, but the demand was clear. If he was to live another day, he'd have to follow through with what fate cast in front of him.

A brush of his coat with his left hand recognized the shape of the wood-handled knife. To get to it under the coat couldn't beat the squeeze of the trigger. Attention would have to be drawn elsewhere. He held out his right palm.

"Will, is it? I'd just as soon have no trouble."

"I bet you wouldn't."

A turn of the palm to all those surrounding swayed eyes. "There's a heap of people in here. You wouldn't want a stray shot hurting any of your friends."

Another giddy laugh meant the mood hadn't been swayed. "Ain't going to be no stray shots. I got you at a dead aim."

The spite in the voice perked interest. He had been in front of a loaded pistol on too many occasions, but it was often for better reason. "And just why is that?"

Eyes piercing eyes, a sense told him reason wasn't a matter of importance. A smirk left from the giddy laugh slowly faded; the Colt's muzzle wandered. It was time to get a surer feel for the hidden knife.

"I've seen too many of you people coming here," said Will. "More than I wanted to see. You come here to get what you ain't got back in your home, wherever it is. Thinking this state is as rightfully yours as it is mine." The smirk returned, then curled into a scowl. "It ain't. If I don't put an end to it, then more will come and fill up these hills, looking for what will make them rich when it belonged to me in the first place."

"I ain't here to pan for no ore."

"He said he was looking for a woman," the bartender announced. "A singer in San Francisco."

"San Francisco?" Will repeated with surprise. "Hell, that's where most of them come from at the start." A few seconds' pause had the drunk with the Colt eye his target from head to toe. "You don't look like no singer. Or dancer, neither. What do you want with a singer from San Francisco? She your wife? Likely just a whore that stole his money."

"That's what I asked him," said the barkeep.

A glare over the shoulder silenced the bragging bartender. "That's my business," was the stern reply. The time had come to settle the matter without further intrusion. "You were telling these folks all about tales of yourself that you never really done. If you're half the bragging you've done, you wouldn't be holding a man's pistol on him that ain't done no harm to you." A deep breath was needed to stoke what fire might be inside of Will. "You wouldn't need it."

"What?" Will looked at the Colt. "You think I need it? For a big fellow as you? Ain't been the first time I cut a man down to his size. Even bigger one than you."

"I'm hearing a bunch of talk. That's all."

"Don't let him goad you, Will," came from the side. "Just kill him and be done."

Slowly, Will shook his head and that smirk came back onto that gap-toothed mouth. "I don't need this." He put the Colt down on the table. At last, the half bottle of whiskey was playing the man. Will stood and drew out a long handle from his pocket and carefully opened a blade with a flare-edged point. "Ain't none afraid of you."

When given an even chance, it was best not to return it. The notion of tumbling over tables and chairs wasn't appealing. If fate had put him in a bad way, it now gave him a gift. Allowed the time to reach beneath his coat, he drew the wood-handled knife and brought it to notice. The sight of the long double-edged bowie only cooled Will's smirk for an instant. The posture seemed that of a man more than half full of whiskey.

Yet the distance was within his skill. He'd made it before. As he stared down Will, he gripped the handle loosely in his left palm. The allowance to stand and aim would only last an instant and failure would leave him defenseless. This wasn't the first time he'd made the decision. Confidence gave him the courage.

The second before he threw, Will's smirk shrank when the proper stance to fight wasn't shown. The moment would last no more. Left hand up then down, the handle sliding off of the palm, sending the blade end over end toward its target. The point struck Will's left shoulder. The blade plunged through the coat and into the muscle.

A low wail proceeded Will's fall, crashing over the sturdy table and sending it tumbling in his wake. Shrieks came from the two females. The suddenness paralyzed the rest of the room. The few moments wouldn't last long.

He picked up the fallen Peacemaker and when Will's friends gave thoughts of revenge, a quick point of the barrel turned them into cowards. It was then he turned his attention to Will, who struggled to get to his feet. Upon sight of his attacker above, Will reached with his right hand for the long folding

blade. A boot stomped on the wrist produced another wail.

He bent down and gripped the wood handle and
pulled it from Will's shoulder slowly. Now with lips
peeled back wide from agony, and gasps seizing the
sharp tongue, those gapped teeth were in clear view
all the way up to their skinny roots.

The wound was deep and permanent, but not
mortal. He wiped the blade clean on the wool vest.
Before he left, one more thing had to be settled.
"She ain't no whore."

He rose and turned for the door. The Colt calmly
poised ahead kept any with ideas of rushing him
crowded against the wall. Just as he entered, he
backed to the door and slipped the latch behind
him.

"Who the hell are you, mister?" was the question
from the barkeep. A moment's thought was all he
needed to decide that there was no good to come
from answering.

The storm still raged. The runoff would wash
away hoofprints and darkness would slow any posse.
He angled his shoulders through the doorway and
slammed the door into the water-swollen jamb.

CHAPTER TWO

The bell sounded. The signal was meant to announce the arrival of the latest visitors to the city. It also served as an appropriate alarm to those finding rest during the swaying ride from the mountains. Clay Cole blinked at the sunshine beaming through the rail car window into his eyes. When he straightened in the seat, a noticeable difference struck his body. Nothing ached.

He took it as a sign that perhaps what he'd known for most of the last few years may be behind him. Another glance through the window provided more confidence of the notion. In what appeared to be a sloping valley, buildings rose from the horizon like a forest. This wasn't something he'd seen before.

A thrust forward was immediately followed by more clangs from the bell and the gradual slowing of the car. Rustling of articles turned his attention to the rear of the car. Men in finer wear and derbies rose from their seats along with their women in big buttoned gowns and matching hats. When he boarded the car, he hadn't remembered as many folks getting on at the same time. The observation wasn't troubling, only it forced him to wonder just exactly how long ago it was when he boarded. The warmth buzzing through his muscles must have come at a cost of more hours than he had first planned.

The train creeping to a stop cleared his mind and turned his attention to gathering his gear. As the patrons filed by his seat, he couldn't keep from noticing their stares at him. He dipped his eyes to the sheepskin coat, the dark green shirt, the muddied trousers and the tanned hide leggings. The faces which passed by weren't that of a friendly sort, and he again wondered if they had picked up a smell which he himself couldn't discern from those he'd carried most of his life. Just the same, he moved to the end of the bench seat until the car was empty.

After a deep breath to gather the gumption to continue into foreign surroundings, he put on his wide-brimmed hat, lifted his saddle over one shoulder and slung his bags over the other, proceeding with the next step to his new life.

He angled through the door and cautiously stepped onto the metal landing. The thick char of smoke pushed him off the landing and onto the solid wood platform. Unsure which way to go next, he followed the rest of the passengers toward the rear of the train. More and more passengers lined the steps leading beyond the depot. Before he could join them, he had to retrieve another passenger.

He kept walking to the end of the train, past the baggage compartments that were unloaded by the porters, and farther to the last two cars. Two coloreds already had unlatched the cradle and began lowering the large ramp.

"Got one here?" was the question.

Cole nodded what he thought was the right answer. "Palomino." As the big ramp was centered on the ground, Cole leapt upon it and walked into the car. Several mounts stood tethered to a line tied around the rim. He slipped the knot free and led the big blond horse out. It took a moment to realize he was the only one to claim his property. "Nobody fetches their own horse?"

"No sir," was the quick reply. "They's taken to the stable. You taking your'n yourself?"

A scan about didn't show any stable in sight. "Whereabouts?"

The porter showed a wide grin. "I take him for you. Can't ride him in the city. Only them pulling carriages allowed." With the ease of a prickly fingered thief, the porter took the reins from his hand. "Five dollars will keep him out the rain and fed good." The amount didn't sound too out of line. He dug in his pocket and paid the board for the horse. He picked up the saddle, but the porter was quick to shake his head. "No need taking that. Goes with the horse, don't it?"

Cole cast a wary eye, but another wide grin soothed his suspicions. "No need fretting. Stable hands take good care of your stock." The porter took a pad from his front pocket and scribbled a pencil over it. He tore off the top sheet. "Keep this for when you come to claim him." It wasn't without any queasy feeling, but Cole accepted the paper, but not before he stopped his step and drew the Mouton rifle from the scabbard. A final nod was the good-bye.

The way toward the steps he'd seen the others

take was stopped by another question. He faced
about to the porters. "How far is the town?"

The porter who'd spoken before grinned again
and pointed toward the lower street. "Trolley take
you there."

Unsure exactly what was meant, he wandered
around the walkway and went to the stairs. Once
on the lower platform, he couldn't keep his eyes off
the numerous buildings. Without a count, he knew
there were more just in his plain view than in all
of El Paso. The smell was a mix of musty smoke
and stench of spilled trash that hadn't been washed
from the streets. Yet, through those other odors, there
were scents he wasn't sure about. Another clanging
bell drew his attention to the right.

An open train car of slighter scale came down the
center of the paved street. Cole stood in stiff amazement. There wasn't any sign of a steam engine attached to the front or rear. Once it stopped, while
four other riders casually boarded, he was less concerned with getting on than as to how the car was to
manage getting going again.

"Are you going into the city?" asked the capped
man who appeared to be the conductor. Cole's lack
of attention to the question only made for a louder
one. "I said, are you getting on?"

Cole shook his head and squinted at the man
with a cock of his head. "How's this thing move?"

"Cables. They run under the street. Now, are you
getting on or not? I have a schedule to maintain."

Still confused, he stepped cautiously onto the rear
landing with rifle in hand. Being the last aboard, a
jolt threw him against the hand rail. The force angled his head down and he saw the slot cut into the

street, yet couldn't penetrate the darkness to see exactly what lay underneath.

Without the success of a discovery, he looked up and about. More buildings and houses built straight despite an angled foundation continued to pass by view. The further the car traveled, the larger the buildings. Some had as many as six ground-floor windows. However, as more and more stood lined next to each other without much space between for three men to walk abreast, it was the ground which crept into his notice.

As steep as any mountain, the incline seemed sure to slow the car to a crawl, but it never did. Once it crested the hill, the slope on the other side appeared certain to send the car careening into one of the houses so close to the street. It didn't do that, either.

As the conductor yanked and pushed long hand levers in the center of the floor, the car stopped and started as it ferried riders from one corner to another and sometimes where there was no corner. With each stop, the air held a smell which sent a distant memory through Cole's head.

As a youth, he marched beside colored soldiers along the coast of the Gulf of Mexico. It wasn't a pleasant memory. It was an affair which many thought would finally end the States War; it was later discovered to be a month after Lee's surrender. It also would take the life of his father, due to a shot he himself provoked.

He swung his head clear of the memory, but the scent remained in his nostrils. With each slope conquered, another came into view. The ride held more roll than any of those he'd been on while riding horseback through the plains. Yet the further the car

traveled, the stronger the scent. The next time it
came to a halt, he jumped off the landing and went
to a spot where no building had yet been erected. A
green knoll of some size was sure to provide a better line of sight. With the momentum provided from
running down the slope, he proceeded up the steep
hill. The crest in sight, he trudged the last few
strides to get to the top.

A gust full of the scent turned him toward the
source. Below was the sprawl of more buildings of
various colors, and in the distance was water stretching beyond the horizon. Ships with sidewheels and
those of mast and sail wandered about in the vast
sea to destinations unknown. It was then he recognized the taste of the brine in the air. Far off in the
dim light he barely made out the presence of other
stretches of land, but none of the colors which surrounded him could be seen.

His breath tightened with stronger gusts, almost
as a signal that where he stood was the point where
others had upon their discovery of this land. He
lowered his eyes to the port, where even more tall
masts rose from their ships, all standing together
like a forest in winter. Small figures ambled about
the docks, but it couldn't be determined exactly
whether their business was coming or leaving.

In it all, he found himself as he stood years before
when first sighting the Rockies. Despite how long
he stared, he couldn't see it all. Upon that realization, he still couldn't take his eyes off the vision.
Something inside stirred him to wonder about this
town which all had spoken about most of his life. It
appeared what was said was true.

"So, this is San Francisco."

* * *

THE LAW OF THE BARBARY COAST

He took a lazy pace wandering through the streets, even the ones which took considerable effort to climb and keep from stumbling down either back or forward. Most of the footholds were in the moist ground, but as he neared even taller buildings he came upon the surety of wooden boardwalks.

Despite the alluring smell of the sea, he couldn't keep from staring at the hotels and shops with windows of fancy script usually used on paper banners and bottle labels. While standing in front of one giant building, he felt the need to turn and find what was behind him. The same style and size lay there as well, but he couldn't help but watch as the swirling clouds broke and allowed the sunshine to beam down upon him.

"Stay right there. Drop those weapons and put your hands in the air!"

The order was loud and firm. The idea of turning to point the rifle at the voice quickly faded once he noticed that the shocked faces which had stopped to gaze at him were the same as those that had been on the train. Unsure of the exact purpose of the order, to fight and hope to leave town in a flurry of bullets didn't seem likely. Slowly, he put the butt of the rifle on the wooden boardwalk and let it slip from his fingers.

"That sidearm, too."

Still with the voice in the rear, he knew if he didn't use care removing the Colt from the holster, he might get shot. With his fingertips, he lifted the pistol from the holster and gently let it fall on the boards with a thud.

"Now, turn around and let me get a good look at you."

Cole complied, heaving a breath, unsure if he was

about to watch the bullet that would kill him fly. Instead, he saw a dress-coated man in a slouch hat holding a shotgun. "What I done?" he asked, with the desire not to hear any mention of his past.

"Broke the ordinance of carrying firearms into town. I'm here to confiscate them and take you in until we find out just who you are."

The law wasn't unheard of in his travels. Other frontier towns had taken up the ban. Usually, he avoided the surrender of his weapons by avoiding those with badges pinned to their coats, but the man in front of him didn't have one. "You the law here?"

The shotgun toter only shook his head, bending to pick up the guns, all the while keeping an eye and the double-barrel trained on Cole. "Vigilance Committee. And I'll take that knife, too."

Cole took the bowie knife from the sheath and handed it butt first. "What?"

"A sworn member to keep the vagrants and undesirables off our streets." He tucked the pistol in his belt and cradled the Mouton rifle while still steadying the shotgun. "All right. Let's march. Straight ahead until I tell you different."

Once again in no position to argue, Cole complied. He walked with the shotgun at his back, uncomfortable with the gawking sneers from passersby, no doubt thinking he was a captured criminal of known repute despite not knowing his name. During his life he had done many deeds which might make him fill that bill. However, he had an urge to shout out to them he was not what they thought. Never had he robbed a man of property who hadn't tried to take his. Only on occasions of defending himself or the defenseless did he end another's life, either in uniform or out. So many years had passed since he lost his senses to corn whiskey, he wasn't exactly sure of the exact date. Only the reason. The vision of a lost bride and baby in flames. Again, he shook the thought from his mind.

Upon reflection, perhaps he was what those who judged him with their eyes thought him to be. Even if he thought himself different, it wasn't up to him to present his opinion of innocence. No matter how hard he could shriek, there weren't words which could change the minds of those watching him paraded at the point of a shotgun.

An order came to turn to the right and after several steps up and down two slopes, the command came to stop. The building seemed like all the others. No bars stuck out from the windows and when they entered, he couldn't find the rack of rifles usually present in the law's office. Instead, he was pushed into a hall, where a rusty steel door was open. Inside was the commonly found bunk and bucket. He gradually faced about and saw the slouched hat just before the door slammed him into complete darkness.

CHAPTER THREE

When the creak of the door pulled him from his brief slumber and light showed the masoned walls, the first thought that entered his mind was, How did I find the bunk to lay on in the dark? Accepting whatever fate awaited, he watched as a dapper-suited gentleman in a silver vest and matching bowler stepped in front of another. He didn't see the slouched-hat one who put him in the cell.

"Get up," was the blunt order. The voice was less firm. Wiping the little nap from his eyes, he noticed the ache in his bones had returned. "What is your name?"

Hayes was an often used favorite to mask his own. However, he wasn't in the mood to lie. "Cole."

"Mr. Cole, you are to come with me. Someone wants to meet you."

The image of the red-haired beauty shot into his head. "Who?"

"Really, does it matter at this moment? Or would you rather stay in here?"

The choice was made in an instant. He rose from

the bunk and walked into the hall. The first dapper man walked just in front and to the side. "What brought you to San Francisco?"

Still groggy from the brief sleep, he couldn't think of another answer besides the truth. "Never been here before. Heard a bunch of talk about it. Thought it was time to see it for myself." He took minor pride in not divulging the complete purpose of the journey.

The dapper man chuckled. "As so many before you. Where do you come from?"

"No place at the time."

"Well, where were you born?"

"Kansas," was the quick answer, although he didn't want to speak more about growing up on the plains, nor his mother dying from consumption, his time with his father during the war, or all that he left there.

"I could have guessed." They walked outside into the bright sunshine against the dark blue sky off to the west.

"How you mean?"

"Your manner of dress. You appear fresh from the cow towns of the prairie." The dapper man stepped into an open buggy, sat with his back to the front and opened his palm for Cole to follow. At first unsure, his caution relented and he stepped into the buggy. As soon as he sat facing the front, the driver shook the reins and sent the single horse on its way.

As they went, he again found himself entranced by the surroundings, until another question broke his concentration.

"What are your plans?"

"Plans?"

"Yes, of course. What had you planned to do while here?"

The first reply entering his head was the only one thought of during the whole trip. However, not comfortable with admitting to seeking to spend more time with the singer, he cleared his throat and let his eyes wander to the surroundings. "Ain't for sure."

The dapper man chuckled. "Well, I'm sure you'll find something to bide your time here." The buggy turned a corner, revealing a completely different view of similar scenery. Countless numbers of folks walked beside the streets and a few crossed it despite the carriage and wagon traffic, which didn't slow much. The higher they stood, the smoother the land became. Allowing his attention to be captured by the taller buildings provided a short sanctuary from further questions. Normally not one secure with being taken on a ride without means to leave if he chose, he relaxed in his seat in the knowledge he didn't have a choice. Without any weapon at hand, he wasn't going any place this fellow didn't want him to go.

The buggy slowed, pulling his eyes to the right. A massive, wide building loomed above, taking up the space from one city street to the other. A circular court led to the front entrance. Looking up at the windows that surrounded him on all sides gave him the feeling they were entering the belly of a huge beast. The dapper man rose from his seat as the buggy came to a stop. "This is it."

"This is what?," he replied, following out of the buggy.

"The Palace Hotel," was the frank answer, given as they continued up the single step. A moment was needed to take in the largest structure he'd ever seen. Entranced by watching the clouds run over the edge of the roof, a loud grunt brought him from his daydream. He followed inside, distracted by the colorful awning. Wide glass doors were propped open and he walked through the entrance with prying eyes darting his way.

Once past the comparatively low ceiling, he found himself again awed by a tall arched glass ceiling supported by metal girders, allowing sunshine to beam into a cavernous room. He had to steady his breath. Nothing looked like this in El Paso. When he stopped gawking at the ceiling, he dipped his eyes down to see a long line of tables and chairs with clean cloths already laid out before anyone sat.

The dapper man waved him to follow closely, like an angry mother to dawdling kids. The motion reminded him he'd been brought here for some purpose. When he walked through the aisle between the tables, he still couldn't help feel all the eyes peer into him. None of the patrons looked like he did. All the men wore fine coats and the ladies were in long skirts, light lacy blouses and large hats. As he passed, he increased his step so to leave their inspection of him.

The two men proceeded into a long hall. Once beyond the sunshine that flowed through the glass ceiling, they came to a corner where another broad window showed the various flowers and vines that grew in the courtyard outside.

"This is the man they told us about." The dapper man's voice drew attention to three seated men, two on a small couch, the third on a chair. As the dapper man walked to stand at their side, the eldest

of them, who sat on the couch puffing on a fat cigar
and stroking his graying, neatly trimmed beard,
looked up from a newspaper. He took the cigar
from his mouth and presented a friendly smile.

"What is your name, sir?"

"Cole," the dapper one answered.

The elder seemed perturbed the answer didn't
come from the one asked. "Perhaps you could find
a chair for Mr. Cole, Chester?" The dapper man's
face shrank from the rebuff like a private from his
commander. In little time, a chair was provided.
"Are you enjoying your time in our city?"

"Of what I've been able to see. Spent more time in
a jail cell than looking around."

The frank answer brought some chuckles from all
of them. "Yes, well, they don't like to have men
with guns walking about the streets."

"You know about that?"

The elder man's smile increased. "I know about
just about everything that goes on in San Francisco.
My name is Waterfield, Mr. Cole. Ambrose Waterfield. I am a patron to this community and wish to
see it thrive even beyond what you have seen." He
took another puff and looked to the dapper man.
"Chester tells me that you were detained by our local Vigilance Committee."

Cole shrugged. "Ain't done nothing wrong. Just
was walking the streets."

"Yes, of course. Well, you must observe the local
ordinances about firearms. Those things are best
kept hidden." He took a puff, then glanced at Chester. A quick eye at the dapper man's open jacket
showed the glint of a short-barreled revolver's shiny
steel. "Nevertheless, those laws need to be enforced

less we have undesirables lurking about to terrorize our citizens, especially our women. Don't you agree?"

The suggestion was hard to disagree with. "There are those in every place I ever come across. Normally they just get run out of town."

Another long drag came before Waterfield nodded. "I'm glad you agree."

As if awoke from a dream, all the surroundings became clearer than before. What confused him was what he was doing in all of this. "Agreed to what? What do you people want with me?"

"Hey," said the dapper man called Chester. "You watch your tone to Mr. Waterfield. One word from him and you'll find yourself back in that cell and forgotten that you were ever in there."

The threat wasn't unnerving. Loud boasts of the powerful had been a frequent nuisance. Normally they were from a barking dog which didn't have much of a bite. But without a weapon and completely lost as to where he was, it was best to hold his tongue. Waterfield seemed amused for a moment, then held up his hand to Chester.

"No, no. Let's not hear any more of that. We're here to welcome Mr. Cole." He faced the front. "Mr. Cole, I see by your attire that you are a man of the Eastern frontier."

Not used to that term, he realized he was as far west as he'd ever been. He slowly nodded. "Been most every place west of the Mississippi. Even a few in Mexico."

"Splendid," said Waterfield. "You may be exactly the type of man we are looking to employ."

The word didn't sound right. "Does that mean you want me to work for you?"

"As a matter of fact, it does," Chester piped.

Waterfield drew another long puff. "What do you say to fifty dollars a week?"

"A week?" That amount was normally earned in a month by lawmen with at least ten years experience or the lies to back up such a brag. A second thought took away the dreams of bags of money. Usually the amount was earned by those lawmen at the expense of the law-abiding, by theft or extortion. "A heap of money. What do I have to do for it?"

"Very likely what you are accustomed to doing for most of your life."

The reference again confused him. "How you mean?"

"You appear a man who likely has gotten to this stage in his life by skill with a gun and knife. Perhaps skirmishes with Indians, outlaws, and all those that trespass on the rights of others where they are not wanted. Am I right?"

The guess sent a spike through his spine. Most of his years were spent doing exactly that. It was the reason he came this far from where he was known; he came to escape the very mention of his name and the bloodshed it caused. Still, there was no ground to be gained from speaking too quickly. "Why might that be of use to you?"

"As I said, I am a patron of the community. My uncle was one of the founding fathers of the Bear Flag Republic with John C. Fremont. This land was meant to provide the opportunity for those to better themselves. I believe this is what California was meant for." The conviction on the elder man's face made it hard to disagree with the notion. The lure of a fair chance for a better life had drawn the masses westward, settling the land and spreading the

American flag across the country. Despite his own experiences doling out justice in the form of bullets— into bodies both red or white—the main purpose for all the fighting was to guarantee the rights of all.

"So you still haven't said what you need me for."

Waterfield glanced about at his friends, a gesture normally seen just before an uneasy message needed to be said. "It's come to my attention, Mr. Cole, that a group of, let's us call them, 'undesirables,' have taken up in the hills to the north of here. There are some mines there, and they are infringing on the locals there. Do you understand what I mean?"

The message was understood. A recent incident came to mind. "I think I may have run into some of them you're talking about."

Again, Waterfield glanced about. "Have you? Well, that may show even more proof of your need to join in our little extraction."

More than once, he'd run across a range war. Hired killers sent to run off settlers from land worked for years just for the sake of a few more acres to graze cattle. This didn't seem that kind of fight, though. "What do you have in mind?"

With a relaxed smile, Waterfield leaned back on the couch. "We need you to join a few other men we've been able to assemble and intercede on behalf of those that the land should belong to. I doubt you should run into any real trouble. Most of the ones we're speaking of are a bunch of rabble that can easily be run out of the state," he paused, "or maybe even run back into the sea."

The peculiar offer forced him to ask the obvious. "Ain't there laws here to protect them folks you're talking about?"

Waterfield seemed disappointed at the question.

Slowly, he nodded. "There are laws which allow for these troublemakers to make claim to the land. It is an oversight, in my opinion. However, it is my stance and those of my colleagues that something must be done to set things right."

"Despite what the law says?"

"In this case," Chester added, slightly opening his jacket, "we prefer the law of the gun."

A glance at Waterfield confirmed his compliance. He'd heard the swagger of words like this before. Especially from someone who didn't have to be one of those with a weapon in his hands. Yet, the lure of fifty dollars a week stood more present in his mind. Before he could ask, Waterfield answered the question he was about to spit out.

"I would like to advance you your first week's wages. And, of course, I would expect you to spend a few nights here in our city and enjoy your stay before you set out on this endeavor." An eye was cast at Chester. "I believe the end of the week should be an ample date to start." The suggestion came with eager nods from all heads. "Until then, Mr. Cole," he said as Chester came forward and slipped a hand in his jacket. The motion tensed Cole's chest in reflex. However, when a wallet was revealed, he felt his heart beat once more. As Chester pulled greenbacks from the wallet, his boss continued. "I would be glad to supply you with one of the rooms here in the hotel. Would that meet your needs?"

With cash money being slapped in his palm, and another glance about his surroundings, he felt a chuckle come from his throat. Attempting to be polite and grateful, he nodded and held back his inner wide smile. "Should do."

"Very well, then," said the gray-bearded elder as

he rose from the couch. "I will leave you in the care of Mr. Haspart," he said, nodding at Chester. "He will see to your needs for the trip."

An important item needed to be addressed. "What about my firearms? They was took by one of them toting a shotgun."

"That can be arranged. But, I think it wise to hold them while you're in the city."

"Yes, I agree. No sense having them taken again by those outside our influence." Waterfield finished by raising an eyebrow. An instant passed before he gave a final assuring nod and held out his hand. "It was a pleasure meeting you, Mr. Cole."

He took the man's hand, careful not to squeeze too hard. "Beholding to you for your kindness." As soon as the last word was off his tongue, he felt Waterfield withdraw his hand. The man then walked into the main room with the table and chairs, the other two following him like ducklings after the waddling mother. Cole rose from the chair and eyed Chester, who came to stand next to him.

"There goes a great man."

Cole looked to Chester after the bold praise. "What's he done?"

"You're looking at a man who has turned San Francisco into the pearl of the West." Chester stopped gazing at the elder. "He made a fortune in silver and brought it all here to spend on the city. He didn't have to do that. He could have kept it all and provided for just himself and his family. But, he chose not to be selfish and to provide for others to make this a better place." Chester stood eye to eye with Cole. "Those qualities aren't common to a man in his position. Makes you not want to let him down when he asks something of you." The point made, Chester took a step forward. "I'll see you get a room here."

"Wait," said Cole, stopping Chester. "If I'm to need bullets, then I'll need my rifle back."

"We'll see you get all the ammunition you'll need."

"No," he replied, shaking his head. "What I need ain't regular. It's a foreign-made piece. Don't take no forty-four or fifty caliber."

"What does it take?"

Again, he shook his head. "Can't tell you for sure."

"Really?" was the curious answer. "All right. I'll get you the rifle, but only if you take it to get ammunition and nowhere else. I can't take time to get you out of jail again." With the sharp tone spoken, Chester walked away with the same strut used by most officers. It was then that second thoughts crept into the back of Cole's mind. However, if the matter were as simple as bragged, then he was set to do as he pleased in a city where no one knew who he was, except one red-haired lady.

CHAPTER FOUR

The lure of the city and its curious attractions brought Cole closer to the door where he entered. About to stray from the hotel, his step was stopped by Chester's call. When he turned, a calm face was needed in order not to alert suspicion.

"Here is the key to the room," said Chester, holding the key at arm's length. Eyeing Cole from boots to hat, he continued, "I suggest you clean most of the prairie off of you if you've plans to go anywhere."

Cole accepted the key. Normally he didn't much heed the suggestions of dressed-up dandies, but with a quick recollection of the sneers he'd collected along his way here, he nodded at the soundness of the idea.

"Come on. I'll show you to the room." Chester pointed further into the hall of the hotel. Again, Clay followed the dapper man's lead and observed the same strange stares he'd noticed before. Through the sunshine beamed from the ceiling, they went beyond the sculpted columns and fancy wall paint-

ings to where a long flight of stairs led to a broad
landing where two other flights ascended in oppo-
site directions. Headed in that direction, he again
halted at the call of Chester.

"We'll take one of the rising rooms."

The mention only served to confuse. When he
saw where Chester's finger pointed, he angled his
head to look around another pillar to where what
appeared to be a row of iron-barred cells stood at
the side of the stairs. Unsure exactly what was
meant, he again looked to Chester's inviting hand,
offering the way. A few more looks to the strange
narrow cells and to the hand were needed before he
took a step toward them.

"These will be much faster."

As Chester casually walked to and entered the
narrow cell, Cole stood at the entrance wondering
why this was much faster to get to the higher floors.
He peered up at the thick cables looped through a
pulley at top of the cell.

"Trust me. You'll get there."

With some memories of block and tackles used to
load cargo onto ships, he still shook his head. Yet,
just about everything he'd seen in the town had
been for the first time; he relented and stepped into
the narrow cell, all the while casting a suspicious
eye at the smug Chester. The dapper man slid the
cell door shut. A latch sounded the same loud clank
of jail. A nod to an awaiting attendant in a red tunic
uniform of some military service was the order for a
lever to be thrown.

Once thrown, the cell jolted. Cole's knees buckled
from the thrust of the floor rising. Instinct had him
grab one of the bars to steady his balance. When he

felt air swirl around his head, he looked forward. The grand lobby sank beneath him. A quick glance at Chester only produced a wider grin.

Peeks to the side revealed the upper floors now coming level. Another peek above saw the glass ceiling getting closer. Below, the crowd in the lobby calmly went about the purpose that brought them there without a curious eye, not bothered by the ascent of this jail cell. Floors flew past as if falling to the ground in layers. Of all the inclines climbed, never had he traversed any with the speed he now traveled. The higher they went, the broader the view; the entire lobby was now in sight. Scanning left to right still allowed for all to be seen. Just as he was enjoying the view, another jolt brought the cell to a halt.

Chester unhooked the latch and slid the door open. Once more an open hand led the way. Cole couldn't help a curious peek down, stopping more than once to lean over the rail and peer. The distance resembled many a sheer cliff to which he'd prefer not to return. Chester grunted to bring him into step like a disturbed parent. Cole came alongside, trying not to gawk at the sights like a child.

Few steps were needed to get in front of a door. 421 were the numbers nailed to it. As he looked to the numerals, Chester wrenched the key from his grasp and poked it into the lock. A single twist had the door open.

A bed with wooden posts on all corners was the first welcome sight. He entered, not wanting to charge in, less all he looked at would vanish like a dream. Chester entered quickly, tossing the key on a small desk, then walking to a broad drape.

"How many bunk in here?"

"Just you," Chester answered with a chuckle.

Cole took his eyes off the wide bed and turned to him. "Just me? In all of this?" The idea didn't seem right. He'd spent nights on many a train car half the size with twice the men this room would hold. Still entranced by the idea, Chester found a cord at the end of the drape and pulled it in a motion like that of a cowboy reeling a lasso.

As the drapes parted, Cole stood stunned by what appeared in front of him. The dark blue sky at the top. Vast sea dotted by white curls which came and went. Ships crossing in each direction. As he approached the window, buildings stood crowded together like wrapped in a bundle. Several tall towers poked above like huge trees. He stood higher than all.

"I never seen nothing like this," he muttered.

"And this is just one side. There's just as grand a view on the other side." Chester retreated toward the door. "Mr. Waterfield spent a good deal of money to see you're comfortable." Cole faced about as Chester stood in the doorway. "He's hoping you remember that when the times comes."

About to close the door, Cole stopped him. "When do I get my rifle?"

"I'll have it here today. There's a gunsmith shop at Third and Bellmore. They should have what you need."

"Third what?"

Chester grinned. "Never mind. I'll send a map."

Again, Cole stopped him before he closed the door. "When do we eat?"

Chester raised a brow. "Anytime you like. Just go to the lobby. Enjoy your stay, Mr. Cole."

Without more questions to keep him, Chester closed the door. Still in a maze of uncertainty, the large bed drew his attention like gravity. He sat on the edge, not wanting to soil any of the fine linens. He unwrapped his leggings and pulled off his boots. Not able to stop even if he wanted to, his body fell back onto the soft mattress.

The need to relieve his water brought his eyes open. The strange surroundings pulled him upright. Confused about the darkened room, he scanned about as piece by piece his mind filled in the blanks. A grin cracked his lips. It wasn't a dream after all. Not this time. That notion pulled him from the bed. There was more to learn. It was the reason that brought him to this town.

The urgent need of nature had him poke about in the dark room. A matchbox near the oil lamp soon had the room bright enough to find a narrow door. Once opened, he saw the means needed to take care of his business.

Hunger was the next need to satisfy. He looked about the room and noticed the key. Once sure in his grasp, he left the room and went to the left in search of the stairs. He passed one of the rising room cars. Although he wouldn't have minded another trip, his lack of ability to operate it forced him to walk down the stairs.

In a little time he was in the lobby. The lamps above made the place seem like daylight. With that, his soiled clothes were again on notice. He sought a remedy.

Advice from one of the tunic-adorned servants steered him toward the barber shop. Once more, he found himself in awe of finding one indoors. What other wonders could possibly be found?

A bath, shave and haircut took slightly less than an hour, but with his soiled duds lying crumpled in the corner, he inquired as to likeliness of buying clothes with the advance given. Without having to stroll naked through the lobby, the accommodating apprentices of the barber shop were only so pleased to fetch several pairs of trousers and shirts for the exchange of a few tales of his experiences as a plainsman. The few mentions of Hickock brought wide eyes to the young faces, which encouraged him to tell even more as he tried on each garment. As he spoke, he uttered that other name. The one by which he'd been known to more folks than he cared to know. Despite the admiration it seemed to bring, if handed the chance, he'd take it back.

Clean of dirt, whiskers, and excess hair, be paid for the services rendered and went back into the lobby with the advice of where to go from those he'd just entertained. When leaving the hotel, he saw the gas street lanterns light up the streets with a pinch less clarity than midday. Along the street, he dodged the numerous carriages that traveled the street and those trolleys, which he still didn't understand what moved them.

The aroma of food steered his nose in the direction of the sea. While keeping his balance by leaning to the rear, he marched down the incline until it leveled. When he steadied his balance, he followed the scent to the right. A long red brick building with framed windows three feet high lined the entire side, not five feet apart. All but three of them on the far end were dark.

As he pursued the smell, another one wafted into his nose, but this one wasn't one to follow. A glance into the darkness spotted ropes and masts against the fading light of the west. The pungent odor of rotting fish pushed him nearer to the wall. Each step was met with a creaking scream from the weathered planks.

When he reached the end of the buildings, a pair of doors stood under a lit lantern. Above the door hung a sign swinging from a rod. The carved figure of a bird with long wings was tacked to both sides. Anxious to find what smelled so good, he turned one of the knobs and entered.

The dark, musty, smoky room had two lamps flickering through the haze. If not for the hunger, he never would have kept going, but the enticing smell of bread led him deeper into the den. Through the drifting smoke, he went to what he believed to be the bar. Without a weapon, he scanned the patrons for any threat. Most wore long-sleeve shirts resembling long handles, along with suspenders. Almost all grew long beards or whiskers. On each head sat either a woolen cap or a floppy one with a stiff bill at the front.

He peeked at his own dress. In fine brown trousers and a white shirt with a collar, he'd have felt more comfortable in his own clothes. He shrugged at the difference and went closer to the bar. A broad shouldered barkeep came to serve him, propping a shot glass in front of him. Cole hadn't come to drink.

"What is this place?"

"The Albatross. What do you drink?"

Cole shook his head. "Ain't a drinker. Came due to the smell of food. What you got to eat?"

The barkeep eyed him for an instant, then picked up the glass. "Soup and sourdough is all we keep. Forty cents."

The offer sounded too good to pass, even if it meant eating it among with the stench of sweaty men. However, it wasn't the first time he'd had to eat in crammed quarters. While in Fort Laramie, he had shared many a plate of hash with twenty soldiers in a ten-bunk room.

The barkeep went to the end of the bar, where a large pot sat. He ladled a serving in a bowl, tore a portion of bread and returned in front of Cole, who stuck his nose over the steaming bowl. The aroma was as soft as a down pillow. As he reached for the bread, he was reminded of the fare in a rude tone.

"Forty cents."

Despite taking minor offense at the tone, he complied by sinking his right hand into his pocket. His fingers poked about, but there weren't any round shapes of coins. In fact, there weren't any shapes in that pocket. His heart beat a mite quicker. He tried the other pocket and discovered the same result. With a instant dip of his eyes, he patted his back pockets. He felt nothing but his rump. He looked up at the steely-eyed barkeep.

"Seems I ain't got it. Left my money in my other clothes. I'd appreciate the stake of the meal and I'd be glad to return in the morning."

After a few moments of a mean glare, the barkeep cracked a grin and huffed a laugh. "Stake you to a meal, you think?" The glare returned quickly. "Why you here? Dressed in the clothes you have? You one of these from Nob Hill? Think you'd have a little fun with us on the wharf, have you?"

Cole shook his head. "Ain't like that. It's the

truth. I just got these clothes and left my belongings in my other pants." The honest reply was heard by most in the place, the evidence being loud guffaws.

"Now, I have to sell this bowl to someone with money. The bread's been touched and ain't going to be wanted by nobody. I don't like doing that. So, to help you gather my money, I'm going to have Little John show you the way back to where you came."

Cole looked right. From the dark haze emerged a giant broad-shouldered man that made the barkeep appear small. Without a weapon, and pinned inside stiff clothes, Cole thought it a bad idea to push his luck. He held up his right palm. "I'll leave on my own."

"Oh, you'll be leaving all right, you will," the barkeep chuckled. "Right on your own ass."

The one called Little John charged at Cole, the hands double the size of a normal man. Cole reached to swat those hands from his throat, but the new clothes didn't allow the free movement of arms and elbows. He felt the grasp of a vise around his throat and another taking hold of his britches. Before he could raise his knee to try and disable the giant, Cole felt his body leave the ground. Headfirst he went into both doors, his head bursting them open like a ram. He went faint with the lack of blood to his brain, but the solid street against his face and ribs quickly brought all feeling back, pain spiking through every nerve.

The guffaws were even louder. Able to open one eye, he saw Little John rub his hands together, return inside the Albatross, and close the doors. Only after a few moments did he rise and carefully stretch his aching arms and feel the pinch of an old injury to his ribs. Still hungry, he felt the safe path would be to return to the hotel.

The long walk back up the hill didn't help. With a slight limp, he went up the street, always casting a cautious eye about to see if anyone else might want to have a try at him. When he reached The Palace, he once again garnered attention, only this time from his torn clothes and soiled sleeves. Anxious to get back to his room, he passed by the row of rising rooms and climbed the stairs. On the fourth floor, he quickly found his room. As soon as he reached for the knob, he realized he didn't have his key, either. His heart sank, but just to confirm another burden to suffer, he gripped the knob. It turned.

He pushed the door open. When he entered, he felt about in the dark with his fingers until he found the matches and the lantern. Once the room was illuminated, his spirit was renewed. There, hanging from the knob at the foot of the bed hung his gunbelt and holstered Colt. Against the wall leaned the Mouton rifle. Thoughts of a return to the Albatross swam in his mind, but his wounds needed tending. He needed rest. His first day in San Francisco had been a long one.

His eyes opened as morning broke. An old habit, he silently shamed himself for wasting at least an hour of the day. Only a glance was needed to know what clothes to wear.

He slipped on the dark green shirt over the bandage on his elbow. With the front buttoned, he slipped on the boots. No need for the leggings, not in town. He took the Colt from the holster. He didn't need another run-in with the local shotgun toters walking the street, so he tucked the barrel in his waist. The sheepskin coat, although it would likely bring on a sweat if it was a hot day, would cover the weapon. Certain of his plan, he took the Mouton rifle from the wall and left the room.

He marched with a determined pace through the lobby. The early hour spared him more curious glares. Before he walked out, he stopped at the desk, where another tunic wearer stood guard.

"Bellmore and Third? Where will I find it?"

As soon as the servant saw the rifle, his stoic manner slipped. "Ah, ah. Third Street is four blocks to the south. Bellmore will be three streets over to the right."

Not exactly sure of the path, Cole nodded, certain that if he could find water in west Texas, he could find the gun shop. He left The Palace and strode with purpose in the indicated direction. Just as in the hotel, dawn provided him with the advantage needed to elude watchful eyes. However, the path over the ever-angled ground brought pain to his side, and the lack of food stung the bottom of his gut. Yet he wasn't about to stop. He was saving it. He had two missions to see to before the day was done.

At the last count he had gone the needed distance south. Approaching the street he thought to look at the sign on the corner post. The letters appeared familiar, but he still wasn't sure. So, with little time lost, he headed once again down the sharp slope. Several glances about didn't show any threats, but just the same he kept a steady pace, pausing only to slow his momentum from gravity's constant pull. During his search for any prying eyes, he spotted another of those swinging signs. Once again, there were letters he'd seen before, but he couldn't make out the word. However, the image was one he'd seen almost all his life. He went to the door below the symbol of the pistol.

When he entered, the jingle of chimes announced him to the proprietor, a slim man of short stature with a bushy gray and black mustache that matched his thick hair. Cole nodded in a friendly manner. "How do."

"Good morning," was the polite answer. "What you got there?"

Cole peeked at the Mouton rifle. "The reason for being here." He laid the rifle on the counter between the two men. The gunsmith appeared enamored of the rifle.

"Never seen anything like this." He poked his fingers into the hole on the bottom. "Takes a magazine through here?"

Cole nodded and reached into his pocket, drawing out two of the mentioned devices that held ammunition, but were empty. Again, the gunsmith appeared in a daze from the appearance of the uncommon loading method. After a few moments, he nodded his head and reached under the counter and slapped down a Bible-thick book. With a lick to his thumb, he flipped pages in gulps, thinning out the search to single pages until he found what was desired.

He pointed at an image. "Knew I'd seen something like this. A Remington-Lee carbine. Loaded thirty caliber into a magazine like that, then a bolt action loads the chamber." He shook his head. "But, I haven't seen one with a pump action. Where'd you get it?"

The answer was an often-told story he didn't like to tell. Still, the gunsmith's arched brow was more an accusation than a question. An answer was needed. "A fellow brought it to Texas looking to fight the Mexicans from around the Rio Grande, and uproot a few white settlers while there."

The gunsmith put on spectacles and inspected the lock. "Appears foreign." He faced Cole. "Come from Europe?"

He nodded. "Some place over there. Can't say exactly. But he claimed his family makes them. Mouton was the name."

"Heard of it. But it's not that well known." The two men stood for a moment in mutual agreement, without more to say. Finally, the gunsmith extended his hand. "Nathan Nichols is my name."

Cole took the hand. "Clay Cole."

Once the greeting ended, the gunsmith looked to the weapon with palms out. "What are you needing to be done?"

"Ammunition for it. Had it for a good while now, and every place I been, haven't been able to match up a cartridge for it."

Nichols inspected closer. "What's it take?"

"Can't say for sure. The cartridge is thinner and longer than a forty-five, but it packs a bigger bang, that's for sure."

Nichols nodded. "Most of the foreign weapons do. But, I can't say I got anything that fits this one. The nearest I have would be less than thirty-six. Don't know if it would fit the bore, neither."

Cole let out a disappointed huff. "Ain't much good to me without bullets." Both men agreed in silence at the thought. It took a moment before Nichols looked up with some surprise.

"Bet I could make what you need."

The claim was encouraging. "How long it take you?"

The enthused face faded a bit. With a cock of the head, Nichols drew in a deep breath. "Would take a spell. Have to measure the bore and press the shells from scratch. Then have to smelt the lead for each shell. Have to find the right amount of grains of powder. Could take quite a while."

The explanation couldn't be argued with, but it still wasn't a matter of course to set out on a trail of bandits without a rifle. "More than a day, I suppose."

The guess brought a single chuckle to the gunsmith. "More like weeks. Maybe a month."

Cole shook his head. "I ain't in a habit to leave behind my belongings. Wasn't easy to get in the first place. Wouldn't be something I can replace."

"Well, I assure you I've been in business for sixteen years. It will be here when you come for it."

"Ain't something I can have. Not right now."

"Why is that?"

Since his new job wasn't one to be bragged about, it wouldn't do to spread word of the plan. "I'm going toward the Sierras in the morning. Can't say I'd be of plain mind if I was to make it without the use of a rifle. Especially one that works as good as this one."

The notion appeared to strike a chord with Nichols. He raised a finger, wagging it as he faced about and yanked a Springfield rifle off the rack. "That will give you peace of mind."

Cole took the rifle, with which he was all too familiar. Although the weapon was the issue of choice for the army and was unmatched by any American rifle in distance and accuracy, it also stood as the sole reason for the worst defeat in the Indian wars.

The memory brought a chill through his bones. The rifle was used by the Seventh Cavalry during the attack on the banks of the Greasy Grass. It's single-shot load was good for a skirmish line when the enemy was more than a thousand yards away. However, when the enemy was on horseback, hiding beneath a ridgeline of uneven hills, and charging with repeating Henry rifles, the Springfield proved to be as useless as a slingshot. It was one of the causes for the defeat of the Seventh, for the death of George Custer, why he stood haunted by the memory and on the run to this day.

He shook his head. "Need something that shoots faster."

Nichols took the rifle and placed it back on the rack, then took an 1873 Winchester in hand and placed it on the counter. Cole picked up the repeater, levering the action twice to be sure it was empty, and put it to his shoulder in mock aim.

"Nothing shoots faster than that."

The opinion was undeniable. Cole nodded and faced the shop owner. "Ain't sure I got the money to pay you for it. I only got a small advance. Not enough to buy it outright."

A few moments passed before Nichols rubbed his chin. "Tell you what. We'll call it a loan. This here pump rifle seems worth more than a ten-year-old repeater. Bring it back in one piece, and pay for the cartridges," he said while stacking two boxes on the counter. "When you come back, you can pay me for my work."

The offer was very gracious and fair. Cole cracked a smile at the gesture. He shook Nichols' hand. "I'll be back in two weeks at most. Think you'll be done by then?"

The gunsmith shrugged. "Never done this type

of thing. Looking forward to the try. If all goes right
the first time, could be that long."

"Good then." Cole spilled out the paper money to
pay for the bullets. With a first step, he halted a
minute, thinking it might not be a good idea to
walk in public with his hands full of a rifle and
shells. The idea of marching back to The Palace with
them meant he surely would be spending more time
behind bars. He faced Nichols once again. "Wouldn't
have a crate I could throw over my shoulder,
would you?"

The gunsmith had the exact item needed to haul
the items back to The Palace. Although a bit clumsy,
Cole managed the return trip up the steep inclines
with only a mild pant by the time he was on the
fourth floor. He had gotten what he needed for the
ride the next day. Now nearly midday, the thought
of a meal sounded better than rest. He knew exactly
the place.

With the Colt still firmly tucked in his belt, he left
the room and was out the front door of The Palace.
Recognizing the street in the light of day, he retraced his path from the night before. With the sun
bobbing between the clouds, its heat steamed the
stench from the wood dock to a height beyond the
roof of the long red building. It wasn't long before
he stood in front of the sign with the bird.

A deep breath was needed prior to entry. He
grabbed the knob and slung open the door. Despite
the bright sunshine outside, the interior was still
dark. A look from right to left found the place with
near as many patrons. The same barkeep stood wiping out glasses, but Cole didn't immediately see Little John. With all eyes focused his way, and despite

being in dangerous surroundings, he felt the need for the proper manners of closing the door.

Cautious steps to the bar were met with eyes following his every motion. He inhaled again, just to feel the Colt hidden inside the coat. He placed his left palm on the bar, leaving his right resting at his belt. The barkeep put down the glass and came his way. The darkness and different clothes appeared to cloud any recollection.

"What you want in here? Looks more like you're wanting something from the stables in the north of town." Chuckles not near as loud as in the night came from behind, but didn't appear any threat.

Cole calmly shook his head. "I heard about the soup and bread in this place. Reckoned I'd give it a try."

A crack of a smile came over the barkeep. "In this place? What fool would have told you that?"

With his eyes on the bar, Cole kept a calm tone. "There was a fellow in here last night. Said it smelled mighty appetizing, but he never got the chance to sample none."

The words hung in the dank air. Like a match spark, the suggestion grew like flame touching tinder. The barkeep's brow furrowed, attempting to stare through the dark. "Some dandy-dressed fellow? Came in here without a single coin to pay?"

"That'd be him," replied Cole with a nod.

"Yes, I do remember him," the barkeep said with a laugh. "Had to sic Little John on the beggar." He looked closer at Cole. "So, that's what you came here for?"

It wasn't exactly true, but Cole nodded anyway. "Smelled so good last night, I had to come back."

The barkeep's grin shrank. "That was you?" Cole stood firm, his eyes stiff on the barkeep, who appeared confused. "Why in the world would you come back?"

With a pause, the answer slipped from Cole's lips, with little regard for the consequence. "You know why."

A few moments went by before the grin returned. It quickly became a hooting call. "Little John. There's a man here who wants you." Just as the words spilled into the air, a huge presence emerged from the far end of the bar. Without any club in hand, Little John marched slowly toward Cole. In that moment, it wasn't clear in his mind why he sought such a fight. Nothing he could speak, but an uneasiness had settled in his blood since tasting the dirt of the street. Now, he held no excuse of being bound by stiff clothes. Now, he would test his own mettle.

Little John increased his gait as he neared. Arms stretched from the sides like a broad elm, they closed a path for Cole's throat once more. The reaction came as instinct. When the giant was within a foot, Cole raised his leg at the knee, firing the toe of the boot like a punch to the giant's crotch. The impact was solid.

Little John stopped, his face bloated at the cheeks. As he stepped forward, Cole didn't hesitate, ramming the heel of his right palm into the giant's chin, snapping the head back like a whip. Little John's eyes rolled back in his head. With a disjointed stare at Cole, he tumbled into a chair, then a table, crashing splintered wood about on the floor.

Another deep breath later, Cole stood over the motionless giant. In that moment, a tingle through his nerves gave him the sense of achievement, just like the Bible story of David over Goliath. A moment later he remembered that he still stood in hostile territory. He slipped his hand inside his coat and gripped the butt of the Colt in case any friends of the giant took offense. He faced the barkeep.

"How 'bout that soup and the bread."

Shoulders slumped, the despondent barkeep went to the kettle. When he returned with the steaming bowl and handful of bread, disappointment was etched across his face. When he placed it in front of Cole, he spoke with decidedly less enthusiasm than he had just minutes ago. A glance to the prone Little John urged a question.

"Did you kill him?"

As he gripped the spoon, Cole shook his head. "Oh, he'll be a mite sore, but dead, nah. He will wish to be when he comes to, but nothing I did to him was mortal." He leaned forward and dipped the spoon into the chunky broth. He blew off the steam and shoved in the spoon. The taste had a cream flavor, almost that of sour milk, and the bits of meat were unknown. He looked to the barkeep and those still in awe at the fallen giant. As he ripped the bread, he nodded. "Damn well worth it."

The remark went unanswered. Only the slow chortle from the barkeep kept him from drawing the Colt. Soon, the infectious joy spread to those at the tables and they surrounded Cole.

"What did you say your name was?"

While chomping on the tough bread, he spoke from the side of his mouth. "Call me Clay."

The barkeep offered his hand. "Samson O'Bannion."

Cole accepted the handshake, then tore off more bread. "Has an addictive flavor about it."

"Local tradition on the wharf. Came from the sour milk recipes of the miners back in forty-nine. What is it that brought you here, Clay?"

A shrug was the first reaction. "Heard so much about this town, knew I had to see it firsthand."

"It is the excuse of many. But, be careful you don't get shanghaied. Many of your kind come here only to get drugged and thrown aboard a ship for the Orient." He ended with a single nod. "Another local tradition." Several scoops of the spoon emptied the bowl. O'Bannion quickly took the bowl on his way to refill it.

"Can only pay for the one."

O'Bannion waved his hand. "Any man that can put down Little John gets free fare." He soon returned with the bowl full and more bread. While eating, one more reason for coming to San Francisco came to Cole.

"Ever heard of a woman singer name of Hooper? Vivien Hooper?"

The barkeep wiped out a glass with a rag, placing it in front of Cole, all the while shaking his head. "There's many a singer in San Francisco. Can't say I've heard of that one." He lifted a whiskey bottle to fill the glass. Although he enjoyed spirits in his youth, the effect on his senses wasn't an event Cole wanted to recapture. He held up his palm. "None for me."

O'Bannion's brow raised. "A teetotaler, are you?"

Cole shook his head, not wishing to appear less the brute he projected. "Too early in the day," he lied.

With some disgust, O'Bannion retook the glass and filled it. "Never too early in the day," he proclaimed, throwing the shot down his own throat.

A dip of the bread into the soup and the lick of

the greasy-tasting drippings filled Cole's tongue again. Yet, he wanted to know more. "If a man was looking for a gal like that, where would he start looking?"

The shot glass was refilled. The barkeep bobbed his head. "If I was of a mind, I would start my search on Jackson Street. A number of opera houses along that line." He slugged down the second shot. A loud exhale followed.

"How would I get there?" asked Cole, swiping the bowl with bread.

"Oh, you have to follow your nose," said one of the patrons.

"That be true," replied O'Bannion. "Have to put it well high. Not to smell anything, mind you. It's just that's the way of that society in that neighborhood, with their noses in the air." All present laughed, but Cole was eager to get a better read on the whereabouts.

"Which is the way?"

O'Bannion shrugged. "Well, if you truly must, you go out the door with a turn to the port side. When you come upon Hyde, you keep that same course, going upwind until you come by Jackson. Once there steer starboard. Maintain that bearing. Go by the small houses until you come about where the street bows a bit. You'll see some of the establishments I'm referring."

Cole stood bewildered. "You mind speaking that again in a tongue a man can understand?"

O'Bannion refilled his glass. "You're no seafarer, Clay. I can see that." He lifted the glass with one hand and pointed with the other. "Go out the door. Bear left. Head north on Hyde. Right to Jackson.

Right again. Keep an eye out." He swigged the liquor.

Cole stood, still uncertain of the directions, but the groaning from an awakening Little John signaled the need to be on his way. Cole put a hand in his pocket, but a wave of the hand by the barkeep meant no payment was needed. Words would have been exchanged if not for O'Bannion's constant pouring and swigging.

Cole stepped from the Albatross and into a mild rainfall. He didn't remember seeing any clouds coming when he went in, but not much seemed as it should in this town. Since he couldn't read the signs on the corners, he followed the streets with the help of the locals. The rain increased along the way.

Once on Jackson Street, he poked his nose toward the small-frame houses, some with staircases to the second floor, others with porches no bigger than the benches propped on them. Many had spire roofs, a design he hadn't seen. Most were made from wood planking, while fewer were covered with red brick. As he admired the homes, he spotted a building slightly larger than the rest. When he saw the front with an unusual design, he took the chance to approach. A small room with a caged window jutted from the front facing just to the left of a pair of doors. He came up to the window, where an interior door was propped open. Further inside, a woman swept the polished wood floor.

He had to ask. "Pardon, ma'am." The interruption stopped her sweeping. "Is this an opera house?"

She pushed the hair from her face. "It is. The Pacific Playhouse."

Encouraged, he stood with his nose just short of

the bars. "I'm looking for a woman that works in these type places. Vivien Hooper. She's a singer. Comes from a foreign country somewheres, but she said she works in San Francisco. Do you know her?"

The woman stood, standing the broom straight under her chin with both hands wrapped around the handle. "I've heard that name." His heart beat a little faster. "But she's not here. Never performed here that I know of."

It couldn't be all good news. "Do you know where I might find her?" More than a few moments passed before the woman came closer. Between the drips from the hat's brim, he got to see she was a youthful girl with a pretty face smudged by the toil of cleaning. She paused as she eyed him from the distant safety of the door.

"I can't say where she might be. A lot of players come and go. Some we never see again. If she is in San Francisco, I haven't heard. Why do you ask? Are you a relative?"

The notion made him grin. "No, I ain't no kin. I met her in Montana. I was just looking to see, to talk to her again." Resolved to the fact he hit a cold trail, he tipped his brim to the woman and faced about to return to The Palace.

"Do you want to leave a note?"

The offer twisted him about in place. "How you mean?"

The woman came closer to the bars. Despite the smudges, she had enticing blue eyes he couldn't keep from staring into. She bent to reach under a narrow counter and straightened with a pencil and pad. "I could write a note for you. I'll give it to

Mr. William Abbott. He's very familiar with all thespians."

Cole shook his head. "Well, I ain't sure what religion she is."

The woman curled a corner of her lip. "I don't think you understand. I'll give it to Mr. Abbott. He knows almost every player. If she comes back in town, he'll know where she is. He's a kind man, I'm sure he'll give it to her. So, what do you want to tell her?"

What he wanted to say wasn't for a young woman to repeat, especially in print. Cole thought for a moment. "Just say that I enjoyed her company very much and only wanted to talk to her again. I really liked being with her in Montana, and tell her I enjoyed her . . ." He paused to rethink his words. "Her singing. She's a good singer."

The woman scribbled words onto the paper. "I think I can convey what you're wanting to tell her. What's your name?" Not easy for him to speak, he paused so long that the woman looked up from the paper. "Well, she's going to want to know who this is from. What is your name?"

"Just tell her, tell her Clay."

The woman spoke as she wrote. "Clay from Montana." She again displayed those eyes. "All right. I will give it to Mr. Abbott."

When she folded the note, all that he'd come for was done. Over the rough ground, the cold, the heat, and the hunger, and the thirst, not to mention dodging a few pieces of lead here and there, it was all done. With no more to do, he tipped his hat. "I'm obliged for your kindness, ma'am." Her smile matched her eyes and she again made certain her hair was away from her face. However, he hadn't come this far for a young girl. Certain of that, he faced about, inhaling deep and exhaling in a huff, tucked his hat firmly to his brow and made his way back through the rain.

CHAPTER FIVE

Low clouds brought misty rain. Cole held the reins of the palomino, prepared to walk it onto a ferry ramp whenever it arrived. He scanned about, silently questioning whether he had awoke well ahead of the group or way behind.

The time gave him opportunity to roll a smoke, a habit rarely enjoyed due to the time needed and scarcity of fresh tobacco. With a flip of the saddle-bag flap, he rummaged through the supplies of jerky, hardtack and extra cartridges until finally recognizing the soft leather pouch. Another peek about showed he need not be in a hurry.

With the end of paper pinched between his fingers and thumb, he doused the tobacco as evenly as possible. Once smoothing it with a few pats, he furled the paper, licking the edge to give it stick. After a slight twist on each end, he looked for a match. Once found, a strike against his boot heel brought a spark, then fire and he touched the end of the smoke to the flame. A deep intake was just what he needed. This wasn't going to be a pleasant day.

Provoking trouble wasn't in his nature. He'd seen firsthand what the spreading of bullets caused and the lives it took. In some cases those of the ones that had nothing to do with it. Still, he'd also seen the good that came from it. Another drag felt good, but he wished he'd had some breakfast. Puffing on an empty stomach didn't settle his nerves as well.

He looked to the paper, now dotted with a few drops of rain. It wouldn't last long, so he took another drag, wondering why he needed to do so. Perhaps it was the idea of once again pointing a barrel at another man. In times past he'd done so in the fury of battle. Usually an instant decision in order to save his own life or the life of another. It wasn't an easy choice, but one made too many times before to keep accurate count.

The final drag allowed him time to ponder just why he was standing in this spot. This is what he had become. A hired gun. Never seeking such a fate, he'd been marked as one none the less. So far all it had brought him was an unwanted reputation. A life on the run. The mention of his name pushed him further away until now. This was as far as he could go. Now, he worked a legal job to use those skills against those that had it coming. And it was a good paying job at that. Fifty dollars a week was a heap of money, not to mention the roof over his head and hot food. The offer was too good to pass by. If it meant running off a band of no-goods from land that wasn't meant for them, then it was the price for such pay. He tossed the paper to the puddles on the dock and snorted the smoke.

"Mr. Cole. Have you been waiting long?"

The question faced him about. In duds more suited for a wrangler, Chester sat in the saddle with

a smirk. A quick glance behind him revealed more
dressed the same leading their mounts. Long rifles
and shotguns were strapped to their gear.

"Not long."

"It's good see a man so eager to earn his pay,"
said Chester, dismounting. He extended his hand.
A moment passed before Cole accepted it. He re-
gretted not having breakfast even more.

Chester pointed behind Cole. "We should be on
our way soon." A glance showed a ferry steaming
toward the dock, its thick black plume dispersing
quickly into the low gray clouds. The uncommon
sight made him wonder if it was a bad sign.

"You should meet some of the men." Chester's
voice once again faced Cole about. "This is Charlie
Biggersby. Next to him is Frank Bowers. Tom Perkins.
Omaha Sam Curtis, Bits Taylor, Malachi Sutton and
Bits's cousin Monroe."

None showed the manner of a friendly greeting.
Cole followed the example.

Two toots of the whistle turned all attention to
the ferry. "Well, men, let's get to the job we're being
paid to do and get back here in one piece."

When the ramp was lowered, each man lined up
and walked their mount aboard single file. As each
claimed a spot for the ride, not a word was passed,
not even between the cousins. Cole looked for any
familiar faces. Often a man who would do this kind
of work might have worn a badge at one time. To
the best of his knowledge, reward money for his
hide still stood and he didn't want to be waiting for
a bullet in the back.

Once all riders were loaded, Chester waved his
wide-brimmed hat and the pilot throttled the steam
engine. It wasn't the first time Cole had crossed

water. Rivers were worst with swift currents constantly pulling downstream. However, it was his trip across the Gulf of Mexico to the southern tip of Texas that he remembered most. Just a boy at the time, the trip would be the first time he carried a musket in service to the Union to stamp out of the last of the rebels shipping cotton abroad.

He squeezed his eyes shut at the memory.

A long march across marshy ground and finally up into the hills led to the last engagement of the war. It was then he pulled a trigger for the first time while aiming at another man. The shot missed, but it eventually led to the spilling of blood. Return fire sent a ball into the captain's gut. His father, Robert Cole.

He shook his head to wipe the memory from his mind. The toss of the waves helped distract him as well as send a few of the fellows closer to the side. He smirked at the pale cheeks. It didn't take long for the curse of the sea to jumble their stomachs and let loose the contents overboard. Maybe missing breakfast wasn't a bad thing after all.

About the time the ferry had gained a full head of steam, it slowed and swung around, at first to the side and then to the rear. It was the first view of the shore they were about to land upon. A few thrusts of the engine, and the ramp soon came down. As when they boarded, the party debarked the ferry. When all were on shore, Cole noticed Chester's horse remained onboard. The one-time dapper man stood firm just at the edge of the ramp.

"It's about ten miles to the first camp you'll encounter. Remember what your duty is." He pointed to Charlie. "Mr. Biggersby will take the lead. I instruct all of you to follow his orders as you would

my own." He opened his arms wide apart. "Gentlemen, I wish you good luck, and I'll see you here in
three days." Chester stepped back on the ramp and
waved while continuing back into the belly of the
ferry.

Cole turned to the rest of the men. Most appeared
similar to the type described as the ones they were
seeking. With a deep breath, he resolved the simi-
larity as a professional hazard. Most of those working for the law had the same past as the outlaws
they hunted. It took one to know the habits.

He stepped into the stirrup and steered the
palomino to follow in line with the rest of the party.
Mud only an inch deep slid away from the drier dirt
below. The steep terrain made it hard to gain any
ground. The low clouds seemed to thin the further
north they rode, but the sun still hid behind the
cover. He didn't mind the slow pace. The rear position gave him the advantage of having all he just
met in front of him and in full view.

There were glares from the front, just as he sent
forward. Up and down the slopes, he took notice of
the sparse trees. If he didn't know the sea was but a
few miles to the west and less than one to the rear,
he couldn't tell much difference between this land
and that of the Kansas prairie. During this observation a voice broke his concentration.

"Hey Cole, come up and take point."

He looked ahead and saw Charlie staring at the
front, but there was no mistaking who gave the order. Fearing it not a sound course, he complied as
ordered. A nudge to the palomino's flanks put him
in the center of the group. About to pass, another remark had him slow the horse.

"We ever cross trails before?"

He didn't face Charlie. No telling when they might have met and he couldn't see the good in pressing his luck. "Can't think of a time when that was. Where you been before?" He didn't see any good that would come from asking that question, but it was out into the wind now.

"Wyoming. Nebraska before that. But we been here and in Nevada for the last five years. How 'bout you?"

The truth might spark more questions than he cared to answer. The first lie to enter his head was one he wished he didn't blurt. "Texas."

"Texas?" asked Charlie with the same tone as if Cole had confessed to carrying the pox. "What part?"

Taking longer than normal to answer, Cole feigned interest in the steep grade a few feet ahead, but he needed to reply with some town. El Paso was the one he knew best in the whole miserable place, but it was too near to California and one of these men might have strayed through it. So, he thought of the first one he'd heard of at the other end of the state. "Fort Worth."

"I been there," touted young Monroe. "Me and Bits, both."

Cole closed his eyes for a moment at the odds. When he opened them, he noticed Bits scowling at his relative. Monroe went silent and his eager smile waned. It was either a sign the claim was a lie or a few folks in Texas were likely looking for the pair of them.

Down the grade they rode, each man with a firm grip on the reins to keep his mount's head up, so as to stay in the saddle. As soon as they were at the base of the small crevice, they rode along the bed with Cole well in front. He didn't like to have all eyes at his back, but he didn't miss further questions about his past.

Less than a mile down the bed, he found a grade slight enough to ride out of the crevice. A glance to the sun gauged it at midday. A meal was in order, his first of the day. He stopped the palomino. The rest of the bunch soon surrounded him.

"Why'd you stop?"

Cole dismounted and looked to Charlie. "We've been riding for six hours. Horses need rest and I could do with some food."

Charlie shook his head. "Don't need rest. We ain't but a few miles from their camp and I don't want to be getting there in the dark. We can complete the raid before sundown and set camp after we're done."

"Raid?" The word held a strange tone. "I thought we were running off a band of outlaws. Raid sounds like we're thieving."

"What's the difference? You some preacher? We come here to do what we been paid to do. Call it what you want, but I ain't a-going to be shooting in the dark of night. Too much chance at hitting our own men."

Cole peeked to the east, where the bunch was headed. The plan of a daylight attack wasn't a bad one. He hadn't thought a meal would take much precious time, but another glance showed he didn't have anyone to join his side. Nevertheless, he was hungry. "Won't take much time. Especially if you planning on riding in there, you're going to need fresh horses."

"I ain't planning on riding in. They're in a canyon

further up in the hills. Two more hours in the saddle will get us there with enough time to do our work."

Charlie's increasing tone made the choice to stay put sound even better. "If you don't think you'll make it before sundown, then you best be on your way. But I'm going to rest my horse and have a bite myself. I'll be there in time for the shooting."

A scowl on the appointed leader's face showed his disgust with the answer. "You best be or I'll see you don't get paid." Charlie spurred his horse and the others followed, each pointing their own glares at Cole as they rode past.

Cole went to the saddlebags and pulled out a bag of jerky. He removed the bit to allow the palomino to graze; later he would cup water in his hand for it to drink. However, all the while he didn't let a minute go by without watching his former riding party head into the hills.

With the last crackling bite of hardtack, Cole rose from a squat and rubbed the crumbs from his hands. The stiff cracker was hardly a meal, and the few strips of jerky he would gnaw on later would do little to stop his hunger. However, another glance at the sun showed he best be on his way. The half hour did some good.

He replaced the bit on the palomino and looked to the trail left by the party. Although not anxious to meet up with the bunch, he needed to be at their side when the shooting commenced. He drew the Colt revolver and again checked the load. Confident all six bullets were still there, he inhaled deeply. Another smoke would help settle his nerves, but he hadn't the time.

Once mounted, he steered the palomino for the
rocky hills to the east. Tracks left by the weighted-
down horses clearly marked the trail. When in the
hills, the prints weren't as easy to follow. Soon he
found himself between two paths that spread in different directions. As he sat in the saddle, he eyed
each one and came to the conclusion that the decision to stop and rest while the others rode ahead
had been unwise.

Now he'd have to make his way among ground
with which he was unfamiliar, all the while under
the threat of heavy gun battles threatening to break
out like a thunderstorm. A peek skyward showed
time was wasting. He nudged the palomino and set
off to the right, figuring if the trail grew cold, he
could double back and pick up the other in time.

Cole steered the horse through the narrow passes,
his left hand holding the reins, the right palmed on
the butt of the Colt. If these hills were filled with
desperate men, a bullet whizzing his way could
come from any angle. He had to be ready to return
fire.

Another turn brought him down a steep incline.
Once more, he scanned about the rocks above. The
thick trees and brush poking out from the side
made for good cover for a shooter. The notion his
own party could use such cover for ambush unsettled him. When he last looked at their disgruntled
faces, they weren't in a mood to welcome him back.
A stray bullet might sweeten their slice of any reward Waterfield might choose to award for a job
well done.

Just as the slope came level, the path led him up
another. He ducked the long limbs stretching from

the old trees above, their roots bulging from between the cracks in the stone walls. About to call for
any reply, he immediately seized his tongue upon
thought of the foolish idea, and also the distant
echo of voices. When he listened more carefully,
giggles and splashes could be heard.

A nudge to the palomino with a jerk of the reins
to the right brought him to a thick brushy bluff. Below, seen through the tangle and snarls of branches
and leaves, were two girls with very white skin
bobbing up and down in a small creek. Although he
didn't get a clear view, their slight frames and small
bumps of burgeoning womanhood at the chest made
plain they weren't very old.

Despite taking no offense at the sight of naked
young beauties, this was no place or time for
women to stray far from their home. He nudged the
palomino again and rode through the brush.

The stir of branches snapping brought their attention to him. Like turtles on a log, they plopped below the surface. He made his way to the edge of the
creek and waited. Confident they weren't fish and
had to come up for air, he soon saw the bubbles,
and not long after the heads broke the surface with
black hair draping their faces.

He raised his palms out in an act of peace, not
wishing to frighten them. After another turn under
the surface, they again emerged. "Ain't meaning no
harm. Just wanting to tell you both you ought to get
yourselves back to your homes and families."

One looked to the other. It appeared a gesture
they didn't understand. Maybe he didn't put it in the
right words.

"There are some men in these hills. Mean men. If
they was to find two girls without a stitch of clothes

on, ain't no telling what's going to get into their heads. Now, I'm going to turn my back so you can get out and get dressed."

Once more they looked to one another, then went under the surface again. Cole frowned and shook his head. He didn't know what other words to say to make his meaning more clear. It wasn't for sure if it was their fright at being naked in the presence of a man, which he considered a strong reason, or the fact they appeared only near the age of fifteen, or that they were female. Any could be cause for lack of paying attention. The heads both broke the surface at the same time.

"Listen here, this ain't no game. You two need heed what I'm telling. These men ain't like me. They wouldn't be still on the bank just talking to you. They'd be after you, dragging you from the water, then doing things we shouldn't be speaking. So, I'm going to turn about. I'm thinking you ought to do as told and get back to your home." He pulled the reins to turn the palomino. Just when he faced about, a light voice had him stop the horse.

"Wait," was what it sounded like. He glanced over his shoulder. The one to the right drew the hair from her face. The round face, the eyelids—he'd seen them before. In reaction, he scanned the rocks above and trees surrounding for a purpose he couldn't describe. When his brain forced him to look once more, the Chinese girl had swam closer, while the other stayed put.

"You," she stammered, stopping to consider, eyes rolling about, "take us?"

"Me?" The idea confused and scared him. He'd been around Chinese, but not women, and the fact this one in the water could talk English almost made him think he was talking to a frog. "I . . . I . . . don't know."

Her face appeared confused. Maybe she didn't understand the words he used. Or maybe she did and the answer disappointed her. Either way, the notion didn't sound like a good one. He wasn't a guide. He'd been hired to battle a band of no-goods, not escort Chinese girls back to their home. So he shook his head.

"I got to be going. There's some other men that I'm a part of that's looking for the ones I was just talking about. I'll be gone soon, so it'll give you a chance to get your clothes back on and scamper back to your family."

Before he hindered his own mind any further, he nudged the palomino firmer than before to get up the grade and back through the thick brush. Only a few times did he glance behind. Both of them remained in the water, which was understandable. Wouldn't make sense to march out of the creek with no clothes after just seeing a man. When he got to the rocky path he turned back to the east.

As he continued, he attempted a few more glances through the brush, yet remained determined not to stop and watch them. A bend in the path put him beyond any sightline. A deep breath reminded him that very soon he was about to engage in a trade of bullets with the kind of men that didn't mind shooting at anything moving. The clouds never had broke and the light of day was dwindling. He needed to make his way to that camp.

The path led him around several more bends. Thought was given to reversing his way to take the other path he had decided against earlier. However, the light wouldn't allow him to get very far, nor

allow him to pick up any tracks to help him along.
The decision to stop, eat and rest had now put him
in a bad position.

Another steep grade meant he'd have to dis-
mount. Once afoot, he led the horse through the
brush with right palm on the butt of the holstered
Colt. He ducked through the thicket, steadying
his balance with a firm grip on the surrounding
branches. A gauge of the path ahead meant he'd
have to leave the palomino behind. He tethered the
reins to a limb, drew the Winchester from the scabbard and proceeded into the denseness.

Birds flying up from the trees turned his attention
to the right. The distance between them and where
he stood made him wonder if someone else was
about. He pulled the Winchester hammer back and
froze in his stance, waiting for any sound. He closed
his eyes and listened.

Just as before, he heard the rustle of voices above
the mild breeze through the leaves. Silently, he angled between the trees, the rifle used as a prod
to move the stray stems from his path. Gently he
stepped over the uneven slope, unsure what he was
to discover. About to take another long stride, he
stopped when he heard louder voices, but there
weren't words he understood.

Not wanting to be discovered, he crouched and
edged forward. Once past a few more trees, he
came to the edge of a cliff. Between the limbs, he
peered down to see a stream running at the base of
a small canyon. He removed the hat and put his
chin just above the rim of the canyon wall. Below,
people assembled near the creek. Tents weren't far
away. He couldn't see their faces due to the wide
cloth hats, but was fairly certain most of them were

men, but there were a few slimmer ones he thought could be women. Their voices grew louder. Unable to recognize any words, it hit him like a hammer to the head that this was where those two Chinese girls had come from.

He looked to the right, but the canyon obstructed any clear view. Yet he was certain the reason for their scurrying likely was due to word spreading about his interruption of the girls' washing in the creek. He didn't mean to cause any panic, but if it meant getting those two back to safety, he didn't mind taking the blame.

As he observed closer, he saw the picks, shovels and pans normally found in any mining camp. The discovery was surprising. It'd been more than ten years since he first saw a Chinaman. Coolies working for the railroad was when he first met up with them while trooping for the army.

Their strange ways didn't sit well with white soldiers and many times he witnessed the teasing of the foreigners, pulling of their long braids, and the stealing of their broad straw hats. At the start, he didn't see the harm in the fun. But soon, it turned personal and there were killings. Just as with the native tribes, the act of a mightier force picking on a weaker one for the sake of domination turned his gut. It was when he decided these folks, although different, weren't a threat to white folks. Others saw it differently.

He looked down and noticed the panic seemed to be rising. Even though he could understand the worry for the girls, who he was yet to see, the notion of a single white man wouldn't appear cause to fret. Couldn't have been the first time they'd learned of a rider about, but he didn't see any real plan taking place. Instead, like mice uncovered under a wood plank, they scrambled about as more of them raced from the woods and began running along the stream bank. It didn't make sense. What harm did they think one man could cause?

The answer came in an instant. Just as he realized it wasn't word of him at the creek, a gunshot rang out. A glance right showed one of them lying face-down at the bank, blood oozing from the back. Rapid shots blasted from the trees and more of them fell. Women shrieked, but were quickly silenced by more gunfire.

Cole's breath was sucked out of him. The surrounding brush cramped his arms. He couldn't raise the Winchester. His sleeve snagged on a thorn pinning his arm against his ribs, preventing a draw of the Colt. All he could do was watch as those he rode with emerged from the trees, took aim and blasted away at the fleeing miners.

Charlie, Bits, Frank and Monroe ran into the opening. Rifles aimed from the shoulder, they fired at the unarmed Chinese. Cole couldn't breathe and couldn't watch anymore. As the attackers ran after the rest, he struggled against the grasp of the brush, finally tearing his sleeve, the thorn scratching his arm. He ran through the woods, snapping branches in his wake.

More shots rippled through the air. He heard the thunk each time a bullet found a victim. When he came upon the horse, he didn't have time to un-tether the reins and lead it back down the steep grade.

He ran past it with the rifle in both hands, ready to fire. When he got to the rocky path he saw the two girls, in soiled white shirts and trousers running toward the mining camp. It would be seconds before Charlie and the bunch came about.

He ran down the slope, turning his shoulder as a ram against the tangle of limbs. Thorns again brushed his arm and snagged in the bail of the Winchester repeater. The rifle was torn from his grasp. As more gunfire rang out, one of the girls ran away from the sound, but the one who dared talk to him stood her ground in confusion.

Gravity pulled Cole down the slope, unable to stop to retrieve the Winchester. Still under the canopy of leaves, he could see the girl standing below. Bullets ripped into her body. Blood spewed from her front and back. Cole's lack of breath kept him from yelling his rage. She collapsed in an instant. With at least four rifles coming his way, their was no point in pulling a pistol to fire back.

He rose and scrambled back up the slope. Sensing the direction of the creek, he ran through the brush to the west. Swatting branches from his path, he came to a part of the creek, but not the spot he'd first seen the girls. A flash of white turned his attention down.

Through the dense growth he saw the last girl, the one who wouldn't come near him. There was no place for her to escape. He ran downslope at an angle in order to cut into her path. Busting through the thicket, he leapt down to land next to her. Her terrified face set her mouth agape to inhale, and certain to scream. The instant before she could, he slapped his hand over her mouth and wrestled the girl into his arms. Instinct brought him back into the thick cover. He could only afford a few steps before the attackers would be along the same path.

With the force needed, he pushed her onto the

ground and lay on top of her in an effort to cover
her white clothes. Although she trembled and shook,
he didn't sense her fight his grip. Likely the terror
had frozen her body. As he heard the rustle of boots
stomping along the ground, Cole hunched his
shoulders over her head. His hand still firm over
her mouth, he put his lips to her ear and whispered,
"Don't move. Don't make a sound."

CHAPTER SIX

The girl trembled in his grasp. Through the brush, he watched the hired killers, of which he was once a part, steadily walk past. He tightened his left hand covering her mouth, his right hand perched above the butt of the Colt. Any noise or motion might bring attention. With each step of the attackers, he scanned to the east. Perhaps if the two evaded notice, he could head for those hills and have a better chance of escape. Just a little farther did the party need stray and Cole could elude them. As the boots and pants legs became harder to see in the dim light, Cole eased his grasp and rose from the girl. While concentrating on the men wandering away, the girl slipped free and bolted back east toward the Chinese camp.

Cole grabbed at her but she was too quick. Her shrieks of fright turned his attention back to the killers. Sure enough, he heard their voices and calls to each other. With armed men charging at him there was little he could do to defend himself with just a single action pistol. In an instant he made a choice.

"Bits, Monroe," he called. "She went that way."

"Who is that?" they both called.

"It's me. Cole. I caught one of the women, but she shook free. I think we can catch her. She's heading west. Back to a creek I saw her and the other come from."

As he spoke, the cousins swatted their way through the brush, never once letting their rifles off aim. "What do you mean? Where'd you see her? And where you been?"

Bits's question came with the tone of a commander. Since he was in no position to take offense, Cole played along. "I'm sorry. I got lost. When I heard the shooting I saw her come back this way, then all of a sudden, she came a-running and I grabbed her."

"Grabbed her?" asked the young Monroe. "What did you have in mind doing that?"

The inquiry only had one answer to serve his needs. "I thought she might satisfy some of us." While Monroe let out a giddy laugh, his elder cousin elbowed his ribs.

"We didn't come here for that. They're animals." Bits faced Cole. "You should know that. Now, which way did she get to?"

Cole pointed into the west. "This way, I'll show you." He took a step but was stopped.

"Wait," Bits ordered, pointing at the ground. "These look like footprints." He knelt to get a closer look in the twilight.

Cole scanned about. "Where are the others?"

Monroe arched his thumb back through the brush.

"Charlie took the rest of them, thinking some of them may have run to the other camps."

"Other camps?" asked Cole, his hand edging toward the butt of the Colt.

"Yeah," the young man replied. "They's plenty of them all throughout these hills. Charlie set out after them since we're done here."

That plan put another in Cole's head. "Well, let's join them. We're not going to find them in the dark." He took a step away until Bits spoke.

"We ain't leaving this one to tell no tales. She may set out to the camps too and warn them. We've got to take care of all of them." Bits put his nose to the ground in order to see, then he straightened quickly. "It looks like she doubled back. Toward them hills."

Cole was out of lies and excuses. If these two picked up her trail, scattering in the dark, there was no sure way of keeping them from her. As Bits got to one knee and with both their weapons pointing at the ground, it was time to make a stand.

"Leave them rifles on the ground and put your hands in the air," Cole ordered, drawing the Colt and pulling back the hammer. Through the dimness he saw both men's eyes widen.

"What are you doing?" Monroe asked, surprised.

"What am I doing?" He shook his head in disgust "What are you two doing? You just murdered un-armed men and women."

"We was ordered," Monroe answered in confusion.

Bits angrily remarked, "They ain't people. They're heathens."

Cole heard the words before. He froze his finger so not to fire, but just the same he couldn't stand

there and listen anymore. He clubbed the Colt over
Bits's skull, sending the man face-first into the dirt.
Monroe twisted about in fear. Cole pointed the bar-
rel at him, petrifying the young man in place.

"I ain't going to kill you. I ain't like that. But,
what you done is no matter of right. There are bodies back there that have bullets in them you fired."
He took a breath, trying to figure what next to do. If
he was to remain alive, he'd have to make certain
these two couldn't come after him. "Drop your gun
belt. With the sidearm in it."

"What you going to do?"

"Do as I say, boy." Cole had to steady his hand to
keep from squeezing the trigger.

"Why are you doing this, Mr. Cole?" asked Monroe as he slipped the belt through the buckle.

Cole kept a careful eye on the piece in the holster.
"There are things that ain't done. Killing folks in
cold blood is one of those things."

"But Bits said those people were stealing land.
Keeping honest white folks from earning a living.
We was just chasing them off. Some of them didn't
run fast enough, is what Bits said."

Again, Cole's head swung in disgust. "Them are
lies you're listening to. Ain't no folks deserve getting shot just for being where they was." Cole
needed another deep breath, the thoughts of his
own ignorance swelling in his head. While a young
trooper, he had taken up arms against the native
tribes he was ordered to fire upon. He took another
breath. Those times were more then ten years old.
He was a different man now and he needed his
mind straight.

Monroe had the gun belt on the ground.

"Kick it this way." While keeping the pistol aim

firm, he bent to pick up the pistol and tuck it in his belt. "The rifles, too." Monroe complied. "Now, take your kin and get out of here. Don't try to follow or I'll just take it as self-defense and commence shooting. You hear me? You listening?"

Despite the setting darkness, Monroe's multiple nods were easily seen. Cole stepped around the pair as Monroe looped Bits's arm around his shoulder. Bending to scoop the rifles and clutch them against his chest, Cole slowly backed away, keeping the pistol poised at the front. With no threat evident, he moved behind the brush and continued to retreat until he could no longer see the cousins.

As quick as a startled snake, he slipped through the limbs and branches, using what sparse light was available to make his way back to the camp. During the run, thoughts swam in his head as to what type of mess he was getting himself involved in. As he felt the grade rise beneath his feet, instinct for the proper direction guided him through the thick growth. Up the incline, he was able to recognize some snapped branches he'd left in his wake. Through the dark, the reflective blond hide of the palomino served as a beacon. At the animal's side, he shoved the Winchester into the scabbard and stuffed the barrels of the other rifles into the looped flaps of the saddlebags. The protruding stocks left no room to mount the saddle.

He led the horse down the grade, then wound around the hill. In the dark, he spotted the white figure lying on the ground. Unable to see very much, he didn't need to in order to know what it was. He knelt next to the body.

It was such a waste. Here lay a dead girl not much older than fifteen by his earlier memory, shot to death because she was different. He couldn't imagine she stood as any threat to folks in this state. Just the same, her kind wasn't wanted among the whites, and so someone thought she deserved to die.

He flared his nostrils and walked away. He hated to leave her, but without means nor the time to bury her, it was best to get on with trying to find the other one before she met with the same fate.

As he rounded the canyon wall, his boots stumbled upon another body. Cautious steps found others. The need to not ignore the carnage pushed him further into the camp. The glistening stream provided the only reflection. He poked his head into the tents. He prodded his hands and gun barrel into the bedrolls and behind supply bundles. He couldn't feel or hear any presence.

He walked to the edge of the woods, whispering into the dark. After so many repetitions, he soon realized it wasn't likely the girl would answer, especially since she wriggled free from him. He abandoned the search, knowing he'd never find her in the night.

Cole retraced his steps back to the palomino, pondering what to do next. Once again, he was forced to reflect, he had put himself smack dab in the middle of someone's else fight. While deciding whether to make his way back to San Francisco, to pursue what he'd come for in the first place, he couldn't get young Monroe's words out of his head. Why was he doing this?

The notion stuck in his head. However, as he considered, another recollection of what Monroe said came to mind. Charlie and the bunch were still on a killing rampage. Sooner or later, they'd find that other China girl. The thought faced him what he believed to be east. He went to the palomino and took the reins, leaving the camp to the dead.

The walk into the brisk air put him in a better frame of mind. Fog settled on the land, and with quiet steps he felt confident to pass without coming across more of the men. With no gunshots echoing through the canyons, he remembered Charlie's plan of not attacking at night for fear of shooting his own men. Dawn was hours away, and that provision could allow him to get a better position among the rocks.

Lack of light and the shroud of fog forced him to crash into the brush and boulders, which were never more than a few feet apart. As he proceeded, he found the ground steepen. Slowly, with a single hand on the reins, he went up the grade, never really certain where he stood. Pushed by the possibility of something happening to the girl, he found the crest of a hill. A moment was needed to rest. As he did, a very weak spot of light pierced through the fog.

He tethered the reins to a small shrub. Drawing the Winchester, he descended down the grade to get a closer look of just who was below in the canyon. He slid on his behind, careful not to rustle too much as he made his way down. More than once did he lose sight of the flame, but angling through the limbs, he was able to sight it again and move closer.

He sensed the ground level. While approaching, he pointed the rifle ahead, thumb on the hammer and ready to pull back. Still in a crouch, he slowly made his way through the brush and trees. He bobbed his head side to side to see the fire, which now glowed through the haze.

He inhaled to ready himself should he find what he expected. He couldn't be sure whether Monroe had had time to warn his partners; if so, they would surely be quick to fire. He gradually rose from the crouch, prepared to charge into the camp. If he could get the jump on them, he'd have a better chance of surviving, and maybe not have to spread so much lead. The campfire shone brightly, its heat burning away the fog from only itself and making for the best line of sight. As he came through the trees, he first looked about the ground near the fire. There were no bedrolls.

The Winchester flew from his hands. The impact that took it came from the left. Cole glanced that way. Hard wood smashed against his jaw. He fell back. On the ground, he rammed his heel at the presence hovering above. A loud gasp meant he'd landed the kick. He scrambled to his feet. Rapid footsteps from behind turned him about. His first focus was a steel edge coming directly between his eyes.

He rammed his hand at the object. The wood handle slapped against his palm. He wrapped his thumb and fingers around it and pushed the ax away from his forehead, knocking his hat to the ground.

His jaw aching, he tried ripping the ax from the attacker, but a punch to his belly dropped him to the dirt. Through the haze he saw the blade being drawn overhead as if to split a log, only it was his head that was the target. Instinct had him swing his legs to swipe the attacker's feet off the ground. Quickly he tried to seize the ax, but another arm wrapped around his throat.

He thrust an elbow behind, popping the breath from the one behind. He grabbed the wrist around his neck, twisting it backward. With the pressure gone from his throat, he threw another elbow at where he guessed the face was; an instant later the attacker collapsed.

The one in front stood and kicked at Cole's chin. A raised arm blocked the blow and busted that one's balance. Within a moment there was no attack. He stood and reached for the Colt. The holster was empty. He frantically searched for the pistol, but spotted the Winchester. Reaching for it, a blunt point jabbed his ribs from the side. His knees buckled and hit the dirt.

Twisted right, he saw the spade knifing through the air at his eyes. He slapped his palm under the edge and ducked under it. A knuckled punch to the gut sent that one back. The moment gave him the chance to grab the rifle, but the ax swung toward him from the left. He slid his right hand up the rifle barrel, his right on the stock. He used the Winchester as a staff, tucking it under the handle. The blade smashed against the rifle, but the ax spun about and the edge became the point of a pick.

Again, it swung down upon him. He blocked it once more, the rifle pinned under the metal head and wood handle. He rolled backward on the ground and onto his shoulders. He kicked his heels into the gut of the attacker, thrusting his legs, flipping the body over him. He sprang to his feet. The Colt lay on the ground. He reached for it, butt in his palm, finger through the guard and against the trigger. He wrapped his thumb around the hammer, cocking the pistol, pointing the barrel at the one he just flipped.

"Stop!"

The voice came from farther in front. Emerging through the mist were a pair of barrels. Cole froze the pistol's aim while watching the gun-toter slowly walk toward him. "You fire that and I can't stop from pulling this trigger." Panting from the fight, he slowly observed the faces of all three men that now surrounded him. He closed his eyes. How would he convince these Chinamen he had come to warn them? He opened his eyes. "I ain't one of them you've heard about."

The one with the shotgun waved the barrels in a motion for him to drop the pistol. If Cole did, there stood no guarantee he wouldn't take buckshot to his chest and belly. The other two rose to their feet and rearmed themselves with the pick and shovel. No longer aiming the Colt, Cole let it droop to his side and finally dropped it.

The pick and shovel were abandoned for rope. While Cole stared at the double barrels, his hands were tightly bound against his back. His knees were kicked from behind, so he knelt before his captor with the shotgun. "You're making a mistake." The rope rubbed into his skin. "I'm alone. Can't you see?" He grimaced from the pain caused by the coarse rope drawn tightly around his wrists. "You fire that at me, you'll bring the whole gang down on you." More rope was looped around his elbows, just as tight as around his wrists. He had an idea of what to expect. If he didn't talk his way out of this mess, and with word spread about their kind massacred a few miles away, it would make sense to take his life in revenge. He shook his head, not only from the pain in his arms, but from the hopelessness of talking to these foreigners. "You don't understand a word I'm saying, do you?"

The one with the shotgun slowly came toward him. Cole stared at the dual muzzles approaching.

His breath quickened as the cold steel neared. Although he'd took lead in his past, he'd never watched it coming. How would it feel? Would the buckshot smash his brain faster than he could feel any pain? He closed his eyes.

"I know what you say."

The choppy, quick English opened Cole's eyes. He inhaled deeply, partly in relief that fate had given him a chance, partly to settle his rapidly beating heart. "You understand?"

"I know how you say. You are one. Not many."

A moment was needed to decipher the meaning. "Then you understand what I'm saying. I'm by myself. But there are others out there bent on killing the whole bunch of you." He rubbed his numb fingers as best he could to keep feeling in them.

The barrels pushed against his chest. Cole stared at the eyes of the one holding them. "You why not come us kill?"

Cole blinked, thinking of an answer that would not provoke a blast through his body. The only one in his head was the honest one. "I don't believe in killing just to kill." The instant he said it, he realized it wouldn't be enough to convince them of its truth. However, with his joints losing feeling, his mind couldn't come about another explanation which made much sense.

The one with the gun paused, eyes darting to the Colt pistol. He bobbed his head. "Gun. You us kill."

Cole shook his head. "I didn't know who was down here. I thought it was the other bunch. I couldn't just traipse in here without a weapon." Although the notion made good sense for him, he realized it didn't sound like much to them. In a moment, he thought what he would think if matters were turned all about. "I don't how to say this to somebody that doesn't talk good English. I don't know no Chinese, but I did come here to help you. There was a girl. A girl that I saw with another. They were swimming in a creek." He hesitated, trying to think of the words needed to put this right in their heads. He peeked to the side. From what he could tell in the haze, their faces didn't much seem ready for reason. "You got to believe me. I came here to find that girl. I ain't one that takes to killing women, especially when they ain't old enough to know no better."

The one to the right rattled words at the one with the gun, who argued back with the same sharp tone. Cole didn't comprehend any of it, but from the loud voices, he gauged it was his life that was the quarrel. His sole hope was that the one with his fingers around those triggers was on his side. The third one barked in at both of them, but it was the one holding his life in the balance upon whom Cole concentrated his eyes.

After the exchange, his stare was matched. The glow of the fire dwindled slightly, making it hard to focus, but Cole recognized an ease of the gun from his chest and that of the brow of the one holding it.

With the swing of one arm, he ordered the other two. Despite their harsh tone back at him, he repeated the same phrase, only louder. Cole watched as the other two went behind him, not exactly sure if he was to expect another punch to the back of the head. Nevertheless, he sensed it was better than getting shot. In a few moments, the tension from his arms ceased.

Like a shower of life, blood tingled through his nerves. He wiggled his fingers to speed the relief.

As control over his arms returned, he brought them slowly in front of him, his hands slowly responding in order to rub the feeling back into them.

The motion alarmed the one with the shotgun, so that the weapon's aim returned to Cole's chest. As soon as he was able, Cole raised his hands in surrender.

"I ain't going to give you no trouble. I guess this was a fool notion. If you let me, I'll leave you be."

Moments passed. The gun did not stray from its aim. The one who spoke words he could understand shook his head.

"No. Here stay you."

CHAPTER SEVEN

Cole was led further up the incline to an open pit of some ten feet. Forced in, he crashed onto the rocky bottom. As if he didn't have enough aches, he lost some skin on his hands while breaking the fall. He turned to face up at his new keepers. "I told you I didn't have no quarrel with you people."

The one who could speak stood at the top. "Here stay you." He stepped away from the top. Now only the fire's glow stood in the way of the night's stars.

With little he could say to change his fate, Cole settled on the ground. Leaning against the pit wall, he tried to rest, but the jab to his ribs still pained him. He closed his eyes, thinking about those words that now stuck in his craw: *Why am I doing this?*

Gunshots tore Cole from sleep. He blinked rapidly, recognizing the dawn's light. Loud shrills of panic crashed in his ears. The pointy Chinese talk filled the air as more single shots boomed about.

Cole stood in an effort to see what was happening. As more shots rippled through the air and cries of agony came high and low, Cole jumped in an attempt to get a better view. He knew the commotion had to be brought by Charlie Biggersby and the bunch. The Chinamen wouldn't be a match for professional killers.

"Let me out of here! Dammit! They'll kill you all. Let me out!" Only shadows from the horizontal light swept over the top of the hole. He moved as far to the left and to the right to get the best line of sight, but neither showed more than the other. "Get me out of here. I can help you." His plea wasn't just for their sake. If he was found in a hole and the mercy he had given to Monroe had made its way back to Charlie, he knew he couldn't expect the same in kind.

Finally, a face shrouded in shadow stopped as it passed by the hole. "Hey!" His loud shout stopped the figure. The single chance to effect a difference pointed his finger. "Guns! Horse! Go get guns on the horse!" The confused face shook. "No, listen. You need guns. Go get guns!" The talk, and likely his loud tone, only made matters worse. "Get me out of here!" The figure disappeared.

Cole huffed in frustration. In minutes he knew there would be no more Chinese and an angry face staring down on him looking for revenge. He jumped again, but the depth of the pit still held him captive. "Anybody listening to me?" he shouted, eyes closed at the top of the hole.

Rope hit him on the nose. He opened his eyes to see the long line stretched from the top of the pit. He grabbed it and pulled. The firm tug was met with enough resistance to give him a chance to climb against the wall. Hand over hand, he yanked, his ribs aching their pain from before. Like trying to reel in a wild bull, the force needed to scale the pit wall pained his arms, but when his hand reached the edge, he released the rope to pull himself out of the pit.

As soon as he got to his feet, he faced left. Thick gunsmoke hovered. Through the thinning shroud he saw Frank kneel and fire a rifle. The shot wasn't aimed at him. He followed the trajectory and as fast as he turned his head, he saw the bullet already had found the one who had thrown the rope down to him. At the dead man's feet lay the Winchester.

Cole ran to the rifle. He slid on one knee, swiping the weapon from the ground, levering a spent shell from the chamber and bringing it to his shoulder. He sighted Frank down over the barrel. The man he once rode with dropped the aim of his rifle, perhaps in confusion as to why a white man would take aim at him. Cole didn't have time to explain, a chance to convince, nor a second chance, should Frank choose to raise his rifle. He fired. The shot found its mark, putting a bloody hole in Frank's throat.

Cole levered another round into the chamber. A bullet ricocheted off the dirt, sending dust up as high as his eye. Cole twisted right. Charlie stood behind the cover of a tree. Cole fired quickly to suppress further attack. His bullet split bark off the tree.

As Cole levered, Charlie retreated behind another tree. "Monroe was right. You've gone traitor. Killing your own."

The words he'd heard before. More than once he'd been told that white men owed a greater allegiance to those of their own kind, no matter the killing of innocents. When he was a trooper, the thought pushed him further away from the oath he took. As a scout, he settled the notion in his gut that he was just leading the army where they asked to be taken, and faced away from the spilling of blood. The day Custer went into the Greasy Grass was the day when he himself would be branded against his country. Whether right or wrong, he had to do what his senses told him was the right course. "Never signed up to kill people in cold blood," he yelled, squeezing off another round.

"I'm going to remember this, Cole," Charlie yelled. "You ain't getting paid." An errant shot boomed from the tree. "We coming back." Another shot rang out. "We're going to be back." The echo was the voice in full retreat.

Cole didn't waste any lead. To chase after Charlie was a fool's idea. Aside from the likelihood of Charlie waiting in ambush, the real truth was he was just too tired to scamper up and down the hills, not to mention sore from the fight during the night.

Whimpers and cries turned him about. A Chinese woman knelt next to the side of the body of the one who threw the rope to him. It was a sadness he had witnessed before. As she wept, he couldn't help be reminded of squaws in the same act next to the bucks who had been killed in battle or children cut down during an escape. Mourning had no certain face.

The vision drooped his arms. The Winchester swung loosely. Cole stood, his head dipped down, his eyes focused on the ground. Footsteps approaching pulled his attention back to the front. By his best recollection, the one who once held a shotgun at his chest now stood before him, unarmed.

There was nothing to keep Cole there. If he chose, he could have gotten to his horse and gone back to

San Francisco, although he would have had to find another place to stay, but likely could have found a suitable shelter in order to find Miss Vivien Hooper. Instead, he tossed the Winchester in the air, catching the barrel in his hand with the stock projected to the man.

The gesture was not so much a surrender as an enlistment. A small smile grew upon the man, who Cole could now see clearly was not one of many years. The tattered hat and soiled clothes under suspenders were the same worn by any miner of any color.

The man held out his hand. "Ho Yung."

Cole looked into his eyes and sensed an appreciation. He took the man's hand and shook it firmly. "Clay."

The morning was spent gathering the dead. In all, the toll was four—three men and a women gunned down. Cole helped with the bodies, which were brought further into the woods where a camp lay. Not familiar with the custom, linen was draped over them.

Uncomfortable with an unknown tribute to the dead, Cole left to retrieve the palomino. Cautiously, he went back up the hill, and to his relief saw his well-trained horse still tethered to the brush from the previous night. He inhaled and let it out slowly, realizing had he lost the mount, he'd have been stranded in these hills.

He brought the horse back down the incline and removed the saddle. As the others went about their custom, he found his weapons, reloaded them, and retrieved his hat, brushing the dust from the wide black brim. He found an outcropping overhanging a small depression where there was plenty of grass.

While the palomino grazed, he sat on the rocky perch. The view of the land stretched out in a plain surrounded by rocky mounds of more than a hundred feet. It wasn't the prettiest sight he'd laid eyes upon, but compared to the dreary nature of tending to the dead, it was the best view available.

The approach from behind put his right palm on the Colt in the holster. Upon recognition of his new ally, he relaxed his hand and resumed the view of the plain.

Ho Yung settled next to him, offering a bowl of different sprigs and berries with some boiled rice. Without words, he accepted the food, although hardly enough to quell his hunger. He nodded in thanks. The Chinaman appeared struggling with words, but something compelled him to speak.

"Fighter," he said, then seemed dissatisfied with the expression. "Man," he pointed. "Good." Cole grinned in acceptance of the compliment. Ho Yung pointed at him. "Fighter, you good. Old ways."

Cole pinched the rice with his filthy fingers and stuck it in his mouth. Despite being food, the taste was the same as he imagined wet flour. While chewing, he thought about how he came to know how to fight like these people. The memories came so quick, he recalled them aloud.

"Years back. When I was a trooper," he said between swallows. "I was part of a guard detail." He looked into Ho Yung's eyes, who didn't appear to understand every word, but Cole didn't know any different way to speak. "Anyway, I saw one of the Coolies, he was a cook, getting picked on. Didn't think it was right after they, the other troopers, started to punch at him. About the time I thought to put an end to it, that one kicked the hell out of two

of them troopers. He did," he said with a nod. Ho
Yung's face didn't change, but Cole continued.
"When a few others didn't take to getting no guff
from a Chinaman, they drew their sidearms and
were going to shoot this fellow out of spite, just for
defending himself. Well, I couldn't stand and watch
them kill him. If I'd drawn iron against them, I
knew I'd spend the next six months in the stockade,
and that would be at best. So, I told them to stop.
When they told me to mind my own business, I told
them the same. One thing said and the other, and I
found myself in a fistfight."

He stuck more rice into his mouth. After all, it
was food.

"I tangled with a few of them. They took offense,
just like these killers here, thinking they were better
than you people and I shouldn't be taking up for
them. The sergeant, he broke us apart and threat-
ened to bring us up on charges if we finished what
we started." He pinched more rice and a few of
the berries. "Maybe a day later, the China fellow, he
came to me and did the same as you. Only after he
thanked me, he took my hand and showed how
scarred my knuckles was. He opened my hand and
pointed to the heel of my palm, then put it to his
own nose. So to punch somebody without busting
no knuckles."

The clear memory had Cole grinning and nodding.

"A few other times, when it was at night so no
one could see, he showed more ways to punch a
man, how to kick a man and where so to bring him
down with as little fighting as needed."

He shoved the last of the bowl into his mouth,
but didn't let it stop him from talking.

"Do was his name. Didn't know exactly the rest."

"Do?" Ho Yung spoke with a questioning face.

Cole nodded. "Yeah. Do was what he called himself."

"Fook Do?"

The ring to the quick words touched a memory. Cole nodded again and pointed a finger. "That's it. Sounds like it. You know that fellow? I didn't know what happened to him. You know him?"

Like a pot slowly taking to boil, Ho Yung's face grinned, then he laughed and shook his head. "Fook Do not name."

The answer confused Cole. "How could you know? Sure we're talking about the same fellow? A short man, little like you, but sort of bald in front, long black braid?"

Ho Yung kept shaking his head and chuckling. "Fook Do not name." He rolled his eyes and put his hands in front of him. He clasped the hands and faced Cole. "Fook Do," he stammered, mouthing words without speaking for a moment. "Luck. Good." He pointed at Cole. "Luck good to you."

The notion took a minute to sink into Cole's head. "Luck good to me? What are you saying? Like he told me I was lucky?"

Even longer than he took to understand, Ho Yung's face changed to one of confusion. He blinked quickly, then put his hand to Cole's chest. "Want you luck good."

Just as a hammer to the head, the meaning came to Cole. "He was wishing me good luck?" Ho Yung's head bobbed up and down. Cole wasn't sure if the meaning was the same in American, but it did make sense when he recalled how he and the Coolie last saw each other. Cole cocked his head. "So, he was telling me good luck? That does make sense. So, I guess I never did know what that fellow's name was." Cole was taken aback, feeling a bit of a fool for being under the wrong impression for all these years that past. It took a few moments before both men started laughing together. Soon, the giddiness faded.

Cole looked out onto the plain. "You know, those men were cowards today, but they'll be back. With more men. More guns. They won't take to getting licked. Especially by you people." He looked to Ho Yung. "You're going to need leave before they get back."

Ho Yung nodded, then motioned his head and rose. Cole spotted the palomino, and with no fear the horse would stray too far, he followed. They went back to the camp. Ho Yung walked among his people without a hint of sorrow, despite their bowed heads, which Cole took as a sign of them still mourning.

Ho Yung first went to a set of shovels and picks and pointed up a steep incline. They went through some of the brush and soon saw a stream coming from the side of a rocky precipice. Cole got the idea. He shook his head.

"No. I ain't no miner." His new friend tried to give him the pick, but Cole refused. "No offense. It's a nice thing you're giving, if I'm thinking what you are. But, I ain't got the patience to dig in the ground for the few flakes or stones of ore." The two stood in front of each other. After more than a minute, Ho Yung went back down the hill. Cole followed, unsure of what else he needed to say to make his point.

Ho Yung went to one of the tents and slid out a small chest. A few flips of the fingers unstrapped the buckles strapping it closed. When he opened the lid, several canvas bags were revealed. Lifting one of them in his hand, Ho Yung stretched open the top and shook it. Spilling into his palm were nuggets. Some as big as a walnut. He held them out for Cole to see clearly.

Many stories had been bragged concerning the richness of these hills. Cole never paid much attention, since most of them telling the stories didn't seem like the ones mining the hills, and the ones who did admit to mining them never appeared rich from doing so.

Slowly, he picked up a nugget. Not one to know for sure, the sparkling content of the rock appeared genuine. Perhaps the gesture to stay and mine with them wouldn't be such a folly. Nonetheless, it was backbreaking work with days needed just to earn a single day's pay. And then there would be those long stretches of days when nothing was found. That was his luck. That was what he had known.

He tried to return the nugget, but Ho Yung refused to take it by shaking his head and holding up his palm. Then he pointed at Cole.

"No, I can't take this."

Ho Yung nodded in a single decided motion. "You keep."

It wasn't just the money the stone meant. Likely, one of that size may bring ten dollars, which was a good week's pay in any job. The thought reminded Cole he'd had one that brought fifty a week only two days before. Still, what that one demanded wasn't worth what it asked him to do. The gesture from Ho Yung was kind and very fair for the little he'd done. It was only a matter of a few feet from where bodies lay on the ground. They could have been the ones that unearthed this ore. If he was to give it back for that reason, then the reluctance wouldn't likely be understood and might bring even more disappointment to this Chinaman. He nodded, tucking the rock into his pocket.

"I'm obliged," he said. "But, you should leave here, too. Like I told you. They'll be back. And it won't matter how many guns you got. They'll attack when you're mining. When you ain't looking for them. You understand?"

Ho Yung first blinked his eyes, dipping them somewhat as a sign of thought. Then he looked at the surrounding hills and finally back at Cole. "No," he said, shaking his head. "Here stays home." He spoke holding his hands out wide, "Us."

It had been an answer Cole heard before. He tried to give Sitting Bull the same message. Although he never had the chance to talk the old Sioux medicine man into returning to the reservation, he expected to hear the same answer.

Cole looked about the hills. There was likely a heap more gold looking down upon them. However, to stay would mean a fight. A fight Cole didn't think they could win. Ho Yung walked back to the camp and Cole followed. As they came to the center, Cole glanced right. Initially, he thought his eyes played tricks, but with a few blinks he focused on the China girl dressed in her soiled white clothes toting two water buckets.

"That's her," Cole said with some amazement. He pointed at her, proclaiming the discovery as he went to her. Ho Yung didn't appear surprised, nor impressed. Cole came near with a smile on his face, relieved to see she was still alive. The girl didn't reflect his mood. He didn't expect her to do so since the last time they were together he was holding her down.

Showing some fear at his approach, she gave him a worried sneer and sidestepped away from him. Only from a barking order given her by Ho Yung did the girl stop. Another barrage of words made her put down the buckets and turn to face Cole, who wasn't sure why she obeyed such an angered voice.

Ho Yung walked to Cole. "Girl," he said pointing at Cole. "You?"

Cole shook his head, uncertain exactly what was being said or asked. "I was just saying that this was the girl that I come after. She was one of them that I saw in a creek . . ." He stopped his speech so as not to be forced to explain exactly how he saw them. Even if doubtful they would understand, it didn't need further detail. "She was one of those girls. The other was murdered where she stood, rest her soul." Ho Yung took the girl by the arm and marched to Cole, pointing at her then at him. "What are you doing? I don't really know her. I was just glad to see that she was still alive."

"Name Luan."

"Huh?"

The Chinaman pointed at the girl. "She Luan." He then pointed at Cole. "Girl you."

All the finger pointing didn't seem right, especially with a young girl in the middle. "I ain't sure what you're trying to say. She ain't no kin to me. I figured she was somebody's daughter. Somebody with you people."

Ho Yung stood still, absorbing what Cole had

said. Like in a trance, he gave the same face as before, when he was thinking of the right words.
"Daughter," he said, holding his hand low like the
height of the head of a child. Then he shook his
head. "No." A few more moments passed with that
same face, ending with yet another point at the girl.
"Concubine."

It was the one word and meaning Cole understood the first time heard. Years in Wyoming during
his time in mining camps had familiarized him with
the practice of Chinese laundry masters renting out
the women they brought with them to the miners,
lonely from being away from their wives, hundreds
of miles away. Most he'd seen were a mite older
than this one, but young just the same. They were
little more than slaves. By the looks of this one, her
face reflected that fate. And a quick glance of the
other faces around the camp showed they didn't
think much of her, either.

Cole shook his head. "Her?" His effort to pursue
the girl's safety somehow didn't seem a worthwhile
venture. "She's a whore?"

Ho Yung almost grinned. "Concubine." He flat-
tened his hand and gave a chop in the air. "Now no
man. Dead. Not girl here. Want no concubine."

A woman standing near one of the hills shouted
out. "She wife to your man," she said, pointing at
Cole's waist.

"I don't need no wife," he answered. "Especially
one that ain't even older than fifteen."

Ho Yung stood for an instant, his face never really changing from Cole's answer. He faced to the
girl and barked out another order. Like a mule,
the girl lifted the buckets and turned about, resum-
ing her duty to the group.

Better sense left his mind. "Wait," Cole said. Ho Yung shouted at the girl and she stopped. Breath left him. It was a fool's idea to even think what was on his mind. The girl was Chinese and was better off with those of her own kind, even if she was treated like an unwanted burden. Yet the idea of leaving her to tote heavy water buckets, not to mention be here whenever Charlie and his bunch returned, would be like leaving the coloreds on a plantation. Certainly, somewhere in these hills had to be a town where she could get work in a laundry. Every place had them and always needed more workers. It wasn't much of a plan, but he knew his gut wouldn't leave him be if he just left her here to be tormented for her past.

"All right. She can come with me. But tell her she ain't my wife. And to do what I tell her."

Ho Yung barked at the girl. She gently put down the water buckets. She went to Cole with the face of a prisoner. Her features weren't as pretty as the girl who first talked to him. This one's face was longer and her eyelids tighter. Still, there had to be a young girl behind that face.

Cole shook his head. Why he hastily agreed to this he hadn't a notion, but it wasn't the first time he'd staked himself to what his better sense told him was a female full of trouble.

CHAPTER EIGHT

She couldn't keep from pacing about all four corners of the outer room. She never liked to wait, especially in a place she didn't care to be in the first case. Her better senses tried to calm her fears and she looked out the window to try to relax.

Below, carriage and wagon traffic flooded the city. Men and women in finer wear strolled about as if they had not a care in the world. If only she could be so light of mind. Further on, she saw the towering buildings yet to be completed. Allowing her gaze to widen, she viewed the harbor. That is where it would stand. Her trip to the city for the plans of the statue were a convenient excuse. Her aging mother wouldn't have to be alarmed.

"Mrs. Rhodes," said the young nurse in a white dress and hair drape entering the room. "He will see you now."

The words stood like a sentence before a judge. However, it was the main reason she had traveled from Baltimore. Picking up her small bag, she went through the narrow doorway and into the office. The nurse closed the door behind her.

The skeletal image on the wall did little to ease her fears. The desk along the wall overflowed with paper. She took it as an indication of the busy schedule she had been squeezed into for this appointment. Other distractions alerted her curiosity. A partition stood in the corner. A magnifying glass on a small table could be for examining small samples, or just to read the fine print of the thick manuals stacked in the adjacent corner. All this sent her worst concerns into her mind and made her heart pound just a little bit faster.

The jangle of the knob behind her twisted her about. The creak of the door was an eerie forbearance. The moment had come. The small-statured man had a decided lean forward, a thinning scalp, a goatee, and thick-lensed spectacles in wire frames. "Mrs. Rhodes," he said in a polite voice, "I am Dr. Cohn."

She accepted his gentle handshake and watched as he tossed a set of papers on the desk and sat in the chair. "Please sit down, won't you." She complied in a small armless chair next to the desk. "Why don't you tell me why you came to see me today."

The reasons were only too fresh in her mind. "Well, you see, Doctor, I haven't been feeling well for some time now. I have found myself very tired recently. As well, I've been more nervous than usual. I don't know why."

"Why would you be nervous?"

The answer was easy to recite. "As you know, there are plans about for the Liberty Statue. I feel very compelled to bring it to this country from

France. There are considerable questions as to how it will be afforded, but it is imperative that this gift be accepted as a show of our patriotism. Part of the reason for my visit to New York City is to seek to chair the committee for funding the project. I suppose it has contributed to my moods."

"You?" questioned Dr. Cohn. "A woman?"

The suggestion of gender competence had been a frequent one. "Doctor, I am a very competent woman. When my father was stricken with his ailment, I took over the Thorsberg Shipping Company. Since his death eighteen months ago," she paused for only a instant, "I have been at the helm of the company and have overseen the doubling of its growth in profit. Also, I have involved myself deeply in the suffrage movement. It is an issue I feel strongly about and find completely unsatisfactory in these modern times. After all, this isn't 1783, it is 1883."

Dr. Cohn nodded with pursed lips, as if in deep concentration over her mild rant. He picked a single piece of paper. "I have reviewed your file. How long have you been a widow?"

Her proud mood turned sullen. Memories of John's death were horribly etched in her brain. When he was shot by his mining partner, Hoyt Larsen, in Colorado, it was his last and sole act of defending her. The bullet was meant for her. That was a terrible time in her life and she wished it could be erased from her thoughts, but it would never leave her in peace.

"It will be four years this coming August."

"I see," said the doctor. "And you have had this anxiety, the nervousness since your husband's passing?"

She listened and considered the question. "I don't know. I don't believe I have felt specifically that way since John died." A pleasant glow waved over her. "As you see in my chart, I have a son. Stuart is my world now. He's every bit as handsome as his father, and if I may admit without bias, he is showing signs of brilliance. I know that one day he will be a successful gentleman, and I couldn't be prouder of him."

Her pride didn't change Dr. Cohn's steely concentration. He looked again at the paper. "I am happy for you, Mrs. Rhodes. However, I don't believe your maternal exuberance can replace what is really troubling you."

"And what do you believe the cause is?"

He put the paper on the desk. "I have seen this type of behavior before in women who have not been with a man for some time. The malady is known as hysteria. A common affliction among women."

His conclusion both startled and bewildered her. "I don't believe I understand your meaning."

"Oh, please," said Cohn. "Don't feel badly. It is a common condition. Your symptoms of anxiety are quite revealing. You see, it has been known for years that lack of stimulation to the female sexual organ leads to a build up of hormones in the blood which confuse the brain. It simply is not natural for women to be without that stimulation, until of course later in life when the change in body chemistry occurs with the loss of reproductive urges. Of course, there is a remedy." He rose from the chair. "Why don't you step behind the partition and disrobe."

Her eyes widened from the suggestion. "Excuse me. You want me to do what?"

"The treatment is easier without cumbersome clothes."

"Treatment?" She leaned back in the chair and found her arms had crept closer to her chest. Despite her confidence in this man, the idea of removing her long dress and undergarments unsettled her. "Dr. Cohn, exactly what are you planning to do?"

A friendly smile creased his lips. "Don't be alarmed. I am a professional physician with a twenty-two year practice. I am familiar with all the latest medical information to diagnose and prescribe treatment for all the ailments which affect the woman."

She nodded. "Yes, but you didn't answer my question."

Dr. Cohn raised his brow in a motion of relenting to a patient's apprehensive inquiry. "Well, the standard procedure is to manually massage the area in a manner consistent with the act of copulation."

She felt her heart beat faster. His causal description left her mouth ajar. She couldn't speak, even if she had the words in her mind able to express her shock. Without any verbal objection, Cohn continued.

"Be prepared, it should be done in a vigorous manner which will relieve the excessive hormones in the blood. This will bring a stimulus to the nervous system which will bring about the natural response a woman receives during carnal relations."

Her body stiffened. When able, she rose from her chair in complete horror. "I beg your pardon. I've never heard such insulting language from a man of profession in my life."

The doctor appeared surprised by her reaction.

"Mrs. Rhodes, please. I assure you, I am only speaking like this so you understand what is best for your condition. If you are not comfortable with disrobing, I can perform the procedure under the dress if you like." He faced away to his desk and reached under a stack of paper to retrieve what appeared to be a small prod with a wire on the end, connected to a round drum with a crank handle. "Or I do have this device, just given to me recently, which when inserted in the area, sends electric impulses to the nervous system. Would you be more comfortable with that?"

She had heard enough. She faced away, her mouth open as wide as her eyes. As she grabbed the knob, Dr. Cohn attempted one last explanation. "I do not understand your position, Mrs. Rhodes. I have women patients who seek out this treatment on a weekly basis." She flung the door open as he continued. "My prognosis is you will continue to have these hysterical sensations without some sort of treatment."

She couldn't allow him to have the last word on the matter. Standing in the office doorway, she turned to face the esteemed doctor. "Perhaps so, Dr. Cohn. However, I am perfectly willing to suffer the result rather than submit to the therapy of a man who is accustomed to putting his hands underneath women's dresses. It begs the question, Doctor, whether it is therapy for you or your patients. With that, I will bid you good day, sir." She left the room in a huff. As she passed the nurse, she couldn't resist a final snipe. "You may have the remainder of my appointment."

Careful while descending the stairs in her haste to escape the humiliation, she exited the front door and took a few steps along the sidewalk. It was there she stopped. She braced herself with a hand on a street lamp.

She ran through the events in her brain, closing her eyes at that man's accusation. For a few seconds she considered his diagnosis. Was she in need of a man? The thought had to be dismissed. The revolting thought that the physical need for intimacy with a man was at the heart of all her troubles was preposterous.

Confident she had regained her balance, she released the lamp and continued along the sidewalk. However, she couldn't rid her mind of the premise. Had she put herself under such a heavy burden of work and duty that she'd forgotten what it was like to be in the presence of a man?

She glanced at the buildings, angling through the pedestrians, catching notice of the glares from those gentlemen and ladies in finer wear as to why she would be on the sidewalk without proper escort. Walking alone along a busy street suggested either impropriety of profession or inability to procure a gentleman. Initially, she dismissed the idea. Only when that idea didn't leave her mind did she consider its merit.

That made her stop. Could it be true? A shop window drew her closer. She concentrated on her reflection. Her features didn't appear changed, but in a few months she would turn thirty years old. Middle-aged women weren't desired by eligible gentleman. She removed her glove and ran her fingers along her cheek. Despite the smooth touch, perhaps wrinkles weren't far away in her future. This did little to buoy her mood.

When she again thought of John, it reminded her

of the last moments they shared. When those terrible events unfolded, it was only the presence of another man that made the ordeal survivable. It was that man, a man of the West. Tall, rugged, confident and oblivious to the opinions of others.

A small smile creased her lips. Many a time she had actively sought news about him. Their final farewell at a train depot in the remote mountains of Colorado was also a memory she could not forget. She didn't desire to. Her hand crept near her throat. Her fingers found the ruby brooch, the one he returned to her.

While in thought, her eyes drifted about the glass and found another reflection. A crowd assembled across the street. As she allowed herself to listen, she heard a voice call to the passersby. Curiosity faced her around. The mass of people surrounded a single barker.

Unable to ignore the scene, she crossed the street with care and took her place among the people. Handbills were passed while the barker proclaimed the attraction inside. As most were busy reading, she felt the urge to take one of her own, although normally resistant to vulgar displays of promotion. About to take the paper, a single shouted word sent her heart racing.

"Rainmaker!"

She snatched the paper and scanned what appeared to be a copy of a book cover. The more she read, the faster her heart beat with the delightful tingle shivering through her nerves. She looked to the bottom. She didn't recognize the author despite the ostentatious pseudonym. Nevertheless, it stood as the best revelation in her life during these last four years.

Quickly, she went inside. Through a pair of doors, she entered into an assembly hall. At the front stood a slight-framed man who was not very tall. He spoke in a profound manner with a hand on his lapel, proclaiming in a loud voice of some experience in the West. An open chair allowed Claire to listen and bide her time.

During the dissertation she heard things that were familiar to her about the man described. She giggled at the orator's story about his own exploits during a viciously fought gun battle. By her assessment, he didn't appear the type to have performed such daring deeds and was certain most of what was said was fiction.

Finally, the performance concluded. The audience hurried to the table for an autographed copy of the book, and she stood in line as the author penned his name in a scribbly manner, presumably to disguise his actual signature.

Once she came to the front, the author, his head down, spoke in a superior tone, "And whom may I make this to?"

A thousand thoughts flew through her mind, but only her name was on her tongue. "Mrs. Claire Rhodes."

The author dipped his pen in the inkwell, then scribbled her name and signed the cover page. He closed the book and held it up for her to take. She couldn't move her arms, as she was certain as soon as she took it, the encounter would be over. She still had more to ask. When a moment or two passed, the author lifted his head and put his eyes to hers. He was a young man, not unattractive to view.

"Yes?" he asked. "Was there more you wanted written?"

Again, she refused to take it. Although anxious to read about the adventure this man boasted about having with the subject, she preferred a more personal exchange. Nothing of any sophistication came into her mind. When the delay became awkward, she felt compelled to blurt out their mutual experience. "I know Clay Cole." The author's features changed, at first making him appear uncertain, as if he had misunderstood. "I said, I know Clay Cole. The one in your novel. The Rainmaker."

Now his face became bewildered and almost frightened. Like a thief that had been found out. No longer was he the only person in the room to have experienced being with this now legendary frontiersman. "You do?"

She nodded. "Four years ago. In western Colorado. Near a town called Platte Falls. A rather treacherous mountain pass. The locals there call it Danger Ridge." The mention widened his eyes, and gradually he rose from his chair. Others in line were either perturbed at the interruption or intrigued to eavesdrop.

"Oh my God," he muttered. "I don't believe it. He mentioned the experience while I was with him." Catching himself in the solitary conversation, he shook his head quickly. "Forgive me," he said, extending his hand. "I'm Richard Johnson."

"Claire Rhodes," she answered, her polite smile growing a little from delight.

"Richard Johnson?" spoke the man behind Claire in line. "So, you aren't the real Dick the Dandy?"

The remark soured the author's face. "Of course I am."

The one making the remark left the line and spoke aloud to all that would listen. "The man's a fraud." As he walked to the door a few others joined him. Two women moved up to the table and stepped to Claire's left and right.

"Excuse me," one said with awe. "Did I hear that you actually know The Rainmaker?" Claire couldn't help confess with a nod. "Is he as in the book?"

"As broad-shouldered and as handsome?" asked the one to the left.

Claire let her head bob to one side. "Well, I must admit, there are features about him which are appealing."

"I see you've read my novel," the author proudly said.

"Oh, my, yes," answered the one on the right. "I found him enthralling. And when the both of you fended off Indian attacks for three days, I hung on every word."

Claire looked to Richard. "Indian attacks? Three days? The both of you?"

Richard shrugged in admission of the fabrication. "Literary license," he whispered. He looked to the two women. "Well, I see you two are all that's left of my audience." He penned his name in a book apiece for them and sent them on their way. Before they left, one came up to Claire. "It is so nice to meet you. When is your book coming out?"

Claire peeked at Richard, whose shoulders slumped. "I haven't decided. Perhaps in the future." The answer was enough to satisfy them, as they both exited the hall thumbing through the pages for the section they both admired.

Claire watched them leave, then turned to Richard. "I'm very sorry. I didn't mean to cost you sales."

Richard shrugged again. "It doesn't matter. Most

of the copies are already sold. I was just here by request of the publisher."

"So, you are a success. Congratulations."

A humbleness settled over his face. He picked up the copy he'd signed for her. "All due to him," he replied as he handed it to her.

She accepted it. "I can't wait to read about your heroics with him." She opened her bag, but he held up a palm as a signal to stop.

"Complimentary from the author." She smiled at his generosity. He glanced at the door. "I would enjoy speaking with you further. Would it be permissible to invite you for tea?"

Normally not one to accept invitations from strange men, she couldn't resist to learn more about this man's story with Clay Cole. "You may." He rapidly collected the unsold copies and took his derby from the table. An outstretched arm showed the way. In a little time, they left the assembly hall, stepping over the discarded handbills littering the sidewalk. They went just a few steps to a café with tables and chairs under an awning. Richard pulled out her chair and then took the other. A waiter soon took their order. Once alone, Richard removed a pad from his pocket. "Now, let me ask you. Exactly where in Colorado did you meet him?"

Claire paused, more accustomed to asking questions than answering them. "I beg your pardon?"

Richard looked up from the pad. "Forgive me. I never lose a chance to make notes."

"Reporter," she mused. "It is all right. It was an early ambition of mine." She rethought the question. "I met him near a train depot in Platte Falls. I had come to join my husband." She paused on the phrase. "My late husband."

"I'm sorry. My condolences."

She nodded in acceptance. The waiter returned with cups and saucers, and filled them with tea. She found herself drawn to steam rising from the surface. "Although I didn't know it at the time, he rescued me from a band of men who meant me harm. Rather abruptly I might add." The more she spoke, the clearer her memories.

"I thought him a terrible brute at the time. I didn't get a good look at his face at first, but what I could see was almost frightening. His jaw stern, almost frozen in a permanent scowl. But, later, when I was able to talk to him, I lost my fear of him."

"I did as well," Richard said with a bit of a smile. "He seemed to have that effect on most all that he came across." He shook his head. "I'm sorry, I stopped you. Tell me more."

Claire again looked into the brew. "We spent the first night in a cave. I tried to think how I would escape, but after considering just how much more lost I'd become, I decided to try to coax some words out of him. That's when I saw it. For the first time. I saw his face. I saw him smile. I saw those eyes like the blue sky against that reddened face. It was the first time during the whole trip I felt safe. I don't know why. I had no right to feel that way. But I did."

"And that's when the two of you became friends?"

"Oh no. I would not say that. If you know him, you're never really friends with him. He prefers it that way. I remember him telling me about his horse, and how he never showed affection for it. Because he knew some day that it would stray away or die. He never wanted to be attached to it. I think he treats people in the same way."

Richard's sincere voice pulled her eyes from the

tea. "You know, while we were traveling in Montana, I jotted down notes. Some of them were a bit exaggerated, like how I would want the book I was planning to be. But there were others, more observations, really. He's a very strange man. All during the time when we rode in search of his friend, I remember writing down what I saw in his face. It was a realization that he was the only one who could find him. Both he and the outlaw we were chasing. I saw it in his eyes. The reluctance, almost repulsion for what he'd been sent to do. I remember writing that he was a man trapped in his own abilities. That he was the only man capable of making things right. That he was part of the evil that had been cast to do battle against another evil. Evil versus evil. I don't think he was ever comfortable with the life he's led. Like, he wished for a simpler life. One he could enjoy." A grin broke Richard's face. "So I wrote. Just one of my ramblings."

Claire knew exactly what he spoke. Before she considered the implications of such a familiar act, she placed her hand atop his. This was another kindred soul captivated by an experience with The Rainmaker. When Richard looked down at her hand on his, she removed it slowly.

"And so you were saying, Mrs. Rhodes. I believe you mentioned your fondness for him?"

She almost blushed. Rapidly, her mind recalled when her very life was in his hands. It was difficult, if not impossible, to be indebted to a man who saves one's life. Then there were those other moments. Those brief moments when all her inhibitions left her head as she lay in a naked state beside him. It was more than a mere act of survival in the wet frigid conditions, or so she so briefly thought.

Had it not been for a clap of thunder to remind her of her place, she may have let him, asked him, enticed him to bond with her as man and woman. Quickly, she dismissed the memory, despite its frequency in her dreams.

"Yes, I was very fond of him," she said with a blank stare, then faced Richard. "You know of his past. Of his association with the Custer massacre."

"I am aware of it," Richard nodded. "Though he never spoke of it. I believe that was another demon he wished to avoid."

"Well," she started with her pride resumed, "it is another ambition of mine to see that he is exonerated of all charges. It was President Grant who sent him on that mission to that Indian village. I believe him completely. I intend on bringing it to the attention of Mr. Arthur, if so needed. I did have a brief encounter with Mr. Garfield before he was elected and he promised me he would look into the matter. I lost hope after his assassination." She looked at his face. "But, now with you, and another witness of Clay Cole's company I met, Miss Jane Reeves of Boston, my drive is renewed."

Richard smiled, then looked to his tea. "We didn't even drink a drop, did we?" He removed a watch from his pocket, then noticed her attention to him. "Forgive me. A habit of mine. To be punctual." He closed the clasp. "Wouldn't still have this if not for him," he said, almost in self-thought. He stood and picked up his hat. "I wish we had more time to talk, Mrs. Rhodes. But my train for Chicago leaves in the hour."

"Chicago? You don't live here in New York City?"
He shook his head. "No. My roots are there. Al-

though, at one time I thought of moving here." He reached out his hand.

She accepted the gentlemanly gesture. "Well, perhaps one day, you'll tour Baltimore with your book. I'd enjoy hearing more about that watch with you and Mrs. Johnson."

His face soured. "Chances of that are impossible, I'm afraid." He gave her a polite smile, looking away to the street, then back to her. "My wife is divorcing me. Seems she's had enough of a life with a dreamer."

While still holding his hand, she looked deeper into his eyes. "I like dreamers, Mr. Johnson. I believe it shows the ambition in a man." She paused, unable to bite her tongue. "Seems it is her loss." She glanced down at the novel on the table. In her mind she rationalized that despite the encounter with the doctor that had caused her to feel so degraded, the subject of the book had saved the day and salvaged her trip to New York City.

CHAPTER NINE

Chester walked up the steps of The Palace Hotel. Usually, he wasn't summoned with such a plainly written, direct note. As he entered, he removed his hat and proceeded to the back of the lobby, to the corner where most of the discussions took place. Seated in his customary seat at the end of the small couch, his boss appeared without the usual cigar in his mouth nor with a newspaper by his side. Whatever the subject, it was ever present on his mind.

"You asked to see me?"

"Sit down, Chester."

The order was delivered with a decided mood of authority. Chester complied and crossed his legs in a show of confidence. Something told him he'd need it.

"Have you heard the news?"

Confused by the question, he scrambled his brain, but nothing came immediately to mind. "Have I heard what?"

"Two men have returned. One of them has a split

skull and is doubtful to resume the mission. We haven't heard from the rest of them." Despite the calm tone, the message wasn't meant merely to inform. Chester unfolded his legs and leaned closer.

"What? Who? How could that be possible? I hired those men personally. I can't believe those Chinese could have put up that kind of fight."

A nod from Waterfield meant there was more surprise. He reached down to his side and unfolded a booklet, a thin magazine, which had been creased in the middle. He held it out. "Then no doubt you are unaware of this."

Chester took the magazine. Once he got a clear look he recognized it as a pulp novel, but the cover description gave him no clue as to why it was important. "I don't understand. What is this?"

"I'll spare you the details from reading that overwrought rag, but it holds a very important name. It was just delivered recently to the bookstore here. A vice of mine to read the latest tales of the West written about from those from the East. When I learned of the man described in it, I couldn't help but recall a recent meeting I had."

Chester peered down at the cover and the description of the man. A marshal? He opened the front page and scanned the print for a name. Finally, the two words stood out among the rest. He looked up, mouth open.

Waterfield stared directly into his eyes. "Yes, Chester. It seems you did hire all these men. And into our fold you brought this nefarious Rainmaker."

"I don't believe it," he muttered. "A federal marshal?"

"It would seem that he has left that profession, or so it is implied at the end of that trash. However, it doesn't address what became of him. I think it is reasonable to assume that he has come to our state. In our midst, as it were."

Certain there was more to be said, he was equally as certain he wouldn't be pleased. "You said two men returned?"

"Yes," Waterfield nodded. "I did. Bits and Monroe Taylor. They said Cole took exception to the mission. He didn't believe in what they were doing. He thought it was not right to move those people off the land." Waterfield inhaled and exhaled with a wheezy huff. "Chester, how could this man not know what we meant when we sent him up there?"

The answer took time to contemplate. When he had heard of the man locked up in the jail, he fit the pattern of a drifter who knew how to use a gun. When he first saw him there was nothing to suspect any different. This man Cole appeared ill-educated, short of money and eager to get shelter and a hot meal. It wasn't exactly normal to ask someone if they are a murderer. Most men who came off the plains with a gun strapped to their leg had killed, whether on one side of the law or the other. He didn't concern himself with men's past as long as they were willing to do as told.

However, the more he thought on the subject, he recalled that he did bring Cole to meet with the gentleman now before him. There weren't any clear instructions at that time. The more thought he gave, the less he figured the entire blame was his. About to present that point, common sense seized his tongue. It wasn't wise to deflect blame to one's employer. Especially one as powerful as Ambrose Waterfield. *The* Ambrose Waterfield.

"I don't know, sir," he said, now sitting on the

edge of the chair, legs together. "I'm sorry. It's my fault entirely. I'd be willing to do whatever is needed to rectify the situation." The sincerely delivered confession appeared to have the desired effect. Or so he hoped.

Waterfield sat comfortably reclined against the couch back, his legs crossed. "Now it is necessary to take appropriate measures to settle this matter," he stated again in his calm tone.

Chester gulped. "And, what would that be, Mr. Waterfield?"

"It is now necessary to seek the help of the man we wished to recruit in the first place."

The original reason for disagreement came to mind. "He will probably want to double his price now."

Waterfield looked to the ceiling. "Only if we are lucky. I think he will sense that matters are worse and will demand three-fold as much." Another long intake always proceeded a long reluctance of acceptance. "But matters are worse," he said, now turning his raised brow directly to Chester. "If this man Cole is able to return here, or go anywhere people will listen, and tell them what he knows . . ." he paused. "And whom he knows, and why he knows those people, then there will be considerable political pressure to answer to. Pressure that cannot be ignored or bought and made go away. Do you understand what I am saying, Chester?"

"Yes sir," he replied in a confirming tone. "How do you want me to proceed?"

"Go to him. See to all the necessary details. But make sure he puts an end to this as quickly as possible."

Chester stood. "Right away." He turned about

and started for the door, until stopped by that calm tone.

"Make sure Bits and Monroe are seen to. You understand what I mean, don't you, Chester?"

The meaning was clear. He'd heard it before. "Yes sir, Mr. Waterfield."

The sun crossed over to the west. Cole steered the palomino down a slope, trying to keep both hands on the reins, balance in the saddle and keep his passenger from falling off the horse. The girl wrapped both hands around his waist with a tight enough grip he thought she was trying to lift him. At times, he had trouble breathing, but each time he tried to explain that to her and she'd ease her grip, the next slip of the horse's hoof on the angled ground would cause the death grip to return.

He reined the horse to a stop. It was time for a sip of water and also to survey the land ahead and below for any sign of a settlement where he could leave her. There were none in sight. He uncapped the canteen and took a sip, passing it back without turning his head to her. "You know what water is, don't you. I hope I don't have to explain it." He heard the motion of the water just once. The canteen came back over his shoulder. "All you want?" With no reply, he took another himself, capped the canteen and nudged the palomino.

As the afternoon passed they traveled up and down steep grades. With the slow pace, Cole was anxious to find suitable shelter for the night, but with the girl riding on the rump their chances didn't seem promising.

With the sun setting over the mountains, a vision

from atop a hill of multiple one-story buildings be-low were a most welcome sight. He steered the horse down the grade and to a trot when the ground lev-eled. With the girl hampering its gait, it took almost an hour to get there.

They entered what appeared to be a mining camp around dusk. The first shack they came near had a lantern hanging against a metal plate on the front wall. Cole thought it to be a place to get some food. The girl slid off the rump and he dismounted the saddle.

He tethered the reins to one of the pillars. There would be time later to feed and water the horse, but for now, he had to get some for himself. He took slow steps up the wooden steps to the porch and opened the latch to enter.

Inside was like most mining saloons he'd seen. Unlike ones in cowtowns, these were of more mod-est scenery. There were no card games, nor were there round tables to commence one. Instead, a sin-gle long table, shared by two miners at present, served as the setting to eat a meal. A long plank served as the bar.

He went to the old slim-framed, scraggly bearded barkeep. "I'll have whatever you got to eat and maybe some coffee if it was brewed today." The old man went about to get the order, but before he took two steps, he looked to the door and pointed.

"We don't allow them inside. Carry the pox, they do. Outside is where they belong. I can't serve you until she's gone."

Exhausted, Cole looked to the girl. He was in no mood to argue the policy. "Wait out there." His or-der didn't show on her face, as she remained in the doorway. He pointed and repeated his order. She looked over her shoulder. When she saw nothing, she faced him again. Disgusted, Cole went to her, took her by the arm and marched her down the steps. With firm pressure on her shoulders, he forced her to sit on the steps. He pointed his finger in her face. "Stay here. I'll sneak you some food later. Don't make a nuisance of yourself."

Back in the shack, he returned to the bar. "How 'bout them vittles and some coffee." The barkeep went to the end and returned with some beans and saltpork. It wasn't appetizing, especially since the beans and pork both shared the same tinge of green. However, he'd eaten near-spoiled food before. He hadn't had anything but a few berries and some rice for almost two days. He didn't pack much since he thought he would be back to San Francisco by now. He dug into the beans and scooped them in his mouth.

"So, what's your business?"

The barkeep's question seemed a friendly gesture. He wasn't in the mood for talking, but he didn't want to spur up trouble. "I ain't sure."

"Ain't sure? How's a man not know his business?

Cole took another scoop of beans. The further inquiry perturbed him a bit and since manners weren't needed in this place, he spoke while he chewed. "Because I ain't for sure where it is I am?"

The barkeep chuckled. "Where you are? You're in Cotter, California. Where'd you think it is?"

Wanting a piece of meat, Cole picked one of the pieces of pork from the slop and stuck it on top of the spoonful of beans. "If you say so. Looks like most mining camps to me." The beans dried his tongue. "What about that coffee?"

The barkeep rounded the plank and went to the

pot above a small flame in the pit. As he watched the barkeep, Cole saw the two thick bearded miners looking at him. The barkeep returned with a tin of coffee. Cole took it and slurped the hot brew. The bitter taste put in question whether it was made that day.

Muttering from the slim man caught Cole's notice. "What are you grumbling?"

"This ain't no mining camp. You don't see a bunch of picks and sluice. No men with pans looking for flakes." He pointed at the far wall. "There's a press not a mile from here up into the hills. A dozen four-hundred-pound stamps crushing rocks to get out the ore. Over a hundred men working the shifts earning regular paid wages."

Cole pawed through the beans looking for another piece of pork. By the man's tone, he knew he sparked a flame. It put an idea in his head, but he wanted to keep the thought to himself.

"Don't see many men with pistols on their leg. Why is it you're here?" The question came with a nervous tone. Cole didn't want trouble, and the last time he stood in a place like this, he found himself fighting just to get out. If he was to speak plain, it could settle all nerves.

"I found myself in the middle of a feud between some Chinese and some white folks that didn't want them there. Before this girl got killed, I thought I'd try to find her a place to stay."

A disgusted shake of the head came from the barkeep. "That's what caused all the trouble. These hills are filthy with Orientals. Getting to where a man can't make a decent living due to them always working for slimmer wages. When they passed that law, they should have sent them all back."

The mention seemed strange. "What law?" Cole took a slurp of the overheated coffee. It coated his mouth like varnish.

"The law that kept more from coming over here. That's right. They passed a law in the Congress in Washington to keep the whole of China from coming over here."

The news interrupted Cole's pained swallow. "They did?"

"It's a fact," responded the barkeep with some pride. "It was the law of the land just last year. Never should have let them come in the first place."

Still hungry, but unsure whether he could eat anymore, he put down the spoon, in part due to the peculiar nature of what he was hearing. "They do that to all the foreigners?"

The barkeep dismissed the question as if silly. "No. Why would they do that? The ones that speak English, the Irish, Scots, Germans, Swedes, all them are good workers. Some work up in the mine. Why would they not let them come to this country?"

"Ain't what I saw," he replied, running his tongue through his mouth to pick the bits from his teeth. "When I was with the army, I saw a plenty of them working just as hard as any white men for wages no white men would work for. But they got the job done, and faster than the ones there before them."

"Can't be so," the thin man said. "I heard that before, but I don't believe a word of it. No scrawny Oriental can do the same work as a white man."

Cole tried to remember his previous thought of no trouble, but he couldn't let the comment stay as truth. "I seen it done. And them folks didn't waste their money on no liquor." He paused to think of their other habits. He looked to the beans. "And they cooked their own food." Another point entered his head. "And they didn't go whoring, which kept their wages in their pockets."

" 'Cause no woman would lower herself to bedding those filthy heathens."

The angered response spurred Cole's temper. About the time the comment sank into his head, its truth seemed to fit. Maybe it wasn't such an odd case that the Chinese brought women, girls, to satisfy their needs as men. As he was about to answer about how filthy some white women were that he'd been with, he thought to scan the room before insulting the honor of someone's regard for white women. As he peeked over his shoulder, he noticed the single long table was vacant. His view changed to the open door. The girl wasn't on the steps. "Where'd they go?"

"Where'd who go?" the barkeep asked in a taunting tone.

Cole wasn't waiting for an answer. He moved away from the bar and went outside. A scan left and right saw no sign of her. Down the steps, he thought to call, but couldn't remember how her name was to sound. "Lu . . . Lu . . . Lulu."

He went further to the left. As he walked he looked in the dim light to the other shacks spread about. If someone stood on the front porch, he couldn't be sure to see them. He drew the Colt. Rounding another shack he saw no one. With each step, he figured it was no coincidence the two at the table were gone at the same time. It made him increase his step.

He came upon another shack, but still couldn't see anyone. Frustrated, he looked about the hills. If they took her up into those hills, it wasn't likely

he'd ever find her. A deep breath settled his nerves.
Might it be for the best? He was looking for a place
to put her. An instant's consideration flushed the
thought away. Remembering the attitude of the barkeep, there wasn't likely a man wanting a girl for
any reason other than to fill his needs as a man.

As he scanned about, he heard chirps—only
when he listened closer did he realize those sounds
didn't come from birds. Another step, then another
increased his pace. A slough running at an angle behind the shacks hid from sight whatever might be
on the near bank. Cole took a cautious step. An angled roof came into view. More steps revealed it to
be a latrine. Another step showed there to be two
standing only a few feet apart. He heard more chirps.

Anger stirred his blood. A shape to the left had
him point the Colt. It was a shovel standing with
the spade in the dirt. He ripped it from the ground
and ran down to the latrines. As the chirps sounded
more pained, he holstered the Colt and went between the two narrow buildings. One of the miners
stood while the other lay on top of the girl, her long
white pants crumpled around her ankles.

Just as the standing miner turned his way, Cole
swung the shovel. The back of the spade caught the
miner flush on the side of his head, putting him to
the ground in a heap. The one on top of the girl didn't
slow down. Cole twirled the spade face up and
swung it down to crash into the tattered hat. The
miner ceased his motion in an instant and collapsed
upon the girl. Fearing the man's weight would crush
her, Cole yanked the collar of the man and rolled
him off her. He reached into the dark, aided by her
white clothes, and pulled her off the ground. She

hugged him by instinct. He couldn't help wrapping his arms around her.

Footsteps focused his attention back up the bank. The barkeep and a few others with lanterns came in a rush. Reflex had the Colt in his hand at the front. Two of them with the barkeep held rifles.

"Stay back," Cole ordered, pushing the girl behind him. "If there's any law in this place, these two need to locked up and hung. They forced their peckers in her and that ain't legal. Not even for her."

The barkeep yelled back. "Neither is not paying for food. Take your slant-eyed whore and leave, mister. If we find out you killed them two then we'll be after you and put you to the end of a rope."

Cole reached behind him. The girl wrapped her hand around his. They walked up the hill, with Cole spreading the group by the swing of the barrel. Once they were past the group, he increased his step to get to the horse. The others went to see about their friends. As fast as he could trot, they got to the front of the shack with the lantern on the wall. In short time, Cole mounted the palomino and pulled the girl onto the rump. He steered in the same direction he came into town.

CHAPTER TEN

Finding men of low expectations wasn't difficult. As Chester walked along the inner section of the city, it only took a few stops before he was able to find them. With a smile he approached the two men, crowded to the bar. "Are you two all right?"

"Hell no," replied Bits, rubbing the bandage on his head. "The son of a bitch pistol-whipped me while I wasn't looking." He eyed his young cousin. "Somebody should have been watching."

"How was I to know that he was going to hit you?"

" 'Cause you should have been watching him. You knew we didn't trust him. Him coming from Texas. Can't trust no Texans. They ain't right in the head."

Monroe shrugged. "If you told me that in the first place, I would have been watching. Ain't that right, Mr. Haspart."

Chester grinned. "Please, boys, don't get me in the middle. I'm just glad the both of you are still among the living. Tell me, what did this turncoat Cole say?"

"Oh, he didn't take to gunning down those Chinamen. He said it was wrong. I tried to tell him what I was told. That those people are stealing the land. Heck, I didn't even know until just before we went into the camp. After I thought about it, it didn't bother me."

"Right you are," Chester agreed. "That's what we all have to remember." He signaled the bartender for another round of drinks for the men. "You know, it's a nasty business that must be done. We have to keep that in mind. If we don't defend our culture, then we'll all lose our heritage. It's a matter of being an American." The bartender brought the drinks. Chester lifted his glass as a toast to the comment. All three swigged down the liquor. Chester motioned for another round. "Plenty of that will cure most aches."

"So, what has happened to the rest of them?"

Chester shook his head. "We don't know. Hopefully they've killed Cole and the rest of those Chinese." The glasses were refilled and they threw the whiskey down their throats once more. Chester stared at the bottom of his glass. "So, what have you told people around town about our mission?" He again hailed the bartender.

"Oh," Bits said with surprise. "We haven't said nothing to nobody. You know," he added with an embarrassed grin, "it ain't like it's anybody's business what we're doing. No sir. Nobody knows on account of us."

Chester shifted his eyes to young Monroe. It took a moment for him to understand the same question was asked of him.

"Oh no. Like Bits said, we ain't said nothing. Didn't think it was anything needed known."

Chester nodded, gave them both a grin, then reached for the new round of drinks on the bar. As another gesture of camaraderie, he raised the shot glass and gulped it down with the cousins. A long loud exhale from all three of them signaled satisfaction. "Well, we want you boys back in the saddle and after Cole. If you think you can be ready, I think tomorrow morning can be the time to get you back across the bay and up into those hills."

"We'll drink to that," Bits said with a smile. Chester ordered another round and when they arrived it took only seconds for them to be completed.

Chester wiped a little dribble from his chin. "Oh, boys. I wonder if you'd do me a favor. I have some crates outside I need unloaded. I wonder if you wouldn't mind helping me."

"Sure, Mr. Haspart," Monroe replied. "Seems only fair since you're paying us and all."

Chester nodded and pointed to a back door in the bar. "It's right out here in the alley." He led the two of them through the door. Careful they were close behind, he went to a waiting rail wagon. As they went into the dark, Chester slowed enough to let the two go to the wagon. When they got to it, it was Monroe who first noticed.

"Where's the crates?"

Chester said nothing. Shadows from behind closed in. Bits stood in some confusion, then his back arched with pain. Monroe kept his eyes on Chester. The boyish courtesy wilted from his face in an instant. Monroe glanced to the left. Seeing his elder cousin squeezed with agony seemed to confuse the young man. He didn't move. No reflex to help his own relative. The next instant, the arm wrapped around his front from behind. The blade shined in the moonlight, slicing across his throat. Monroe stumbled, falling to his knees, gurgling from the blood pouring from the slash, his eyes wide and locked directly on Chester, finally collapsing face-first onto the alley stones.

Chester inhaled, satisfied he'd accomplished the initial step in rectifying the debacle and putting himself back in good standing. "These were the two thieves I mentioned to you," he said, speaking indirectly into the shadows. "Load them into the wagon. Take them out into the bay and dump them. Let's be rid of two more members of the Barbary Coast."

The night brought rain. Swaying in the saddle across muddy angles tipped Cole back and forth, sloshing his insides into an unholy stew. The chill of the wind forced more sweat from his brow. He couldn't see, so he let the palomino steer the course. He could barely be sure the girl was still on the rump, spare the few times when her yanks around his belly caused even more jostling to his insides.

When the palomino stopped, he looked to the front. Through the rain, sparkles of light shone through the night. Whether danger waited or not, he nudged the horse to continue. Even if it meant a bullet was waiting, it couldn't bring as much pain as he was feeling at the moment.

While descending the slope, he gripped the horn, his head feeling ever more like a lead weight swinging over the top of his shoulders. As they came down to less angled land, the light grew closer. His guts popping with each step of the horse, he soon needed to find a place to lay, even in the rain. As they slowly approached, he felt the girls hands grip once more, then release. Certain she'd fallen off the horse, he gathered the strength to turn his head. She stood only a few steps from the horse, like a ghostly vision.

With his pained legs screaming from every motion, he slipped off the saddle and fell into the mud. Despite the girl's efforts, it was he that had to muster the strength to stand. He went to the light. The blurry vision slowly focused in the center.

"You all right, son?"

The voice startled him, but he couldn't see the source. He answered to the raindrops, "Need some rest. Pay whatever you want for a blanket."

"What's he got?" asked a higher-pitched voice. He didn't see that one, either. "May be carrying the fever."

Only in short strokes could Cole shake his head. "No. Ate some rotten pork. Just need to let it pass. All I need is to lay down. Pay you what you want."

There were no voices anymore. He stood, his knees bending from the weight, feeling like he was about to snap in half. Each flip of his insides felt like the turn of a blade. After it subsided, he gasped for enough breath to speak. "Ain't wanting to bring any harm. Just need a place to stay."

Rain pelted off his wide black brim. As he stood in a stupor, a hand took his arm, leading him like a child. Only bleary visions of light and dark flashed into his brain. Into the dark he went, foreign hands about his body, pawing at the wet clothes. As he stood, he felt more cold on his sweaty flesh. His head was afire. His bare arms shivered, spreading to his chest like a wildfire. The more attempts he made to stop only brought more violent shakes to his limbs. His legs quivered as if in panic, but instantly they felt the spread of the cold. Unable to see and not knowing where he stood, he bent. His gut expelled the bulging pressure. Cold, wet air never felt so fresh. Unaware of the surroundings, he dismissed his mind from caring. If he should be about friends or enemies, there stood nothing he could do to put up a fight. Rain washed over his body. He felt it all over his flesh.

Able to inhale deeply for the first in a long time, he moved his legs to the lead of an another's arm, only this one didn't have the grip or pull of the one he first felt. The light that had led him to this spot now came back through the distant dark, enlarging with each step. The marshy cold now oozed between his toes.

The light grew bigger, wider, more round, then quickly shrank into a small ball. With his legs moving, his senses cleared. Heat from the side brought welcome relief from the cold, but also stoked the fire that still burned inside his head. Veering from it only brought a tighter grip to his arm. He wanted to avoid the heat and went to the right toward the dark, but the grip pulled him left. He didn't have the power to fight.

He went inside the glow. His bleary eyes only saw the small flame once, but a black blur hung above it. Guided by hands pushing him left and right, up and down, his balance was toppled by the pressure pushing against his chest, forcing him to sit. His butt felt the cold chill of water. Instantly, the shakes returned, vibrating through his nerves. Delusions of drowning made him want to rise, but a firm but gentle push against his chest and a less gruff voice shushed him to comply.

Amongst the glow surrounding him, his eyes kept only half sight. He tried to focus, but his mind swam with thoughts so quick in coming and passing, he couldn't concentrate on the figure now standing in front.

Warmth enveloped him. Every pore of skin opened on his ankles, thighs and waist to the soothing relief of warm water. The warmth rose to surround his belly, then just below his chest. What was happening? Where could he be? He didn't think any longer, having no energy to ponder, allowing his mind to find the answer.

Through the blur, he saw white before him, but it shrank away. There stood a body. Round hips. Thin frame. A female. A naked bosom exposed by the glow. Was it her? "Vivien?" he mumbled. How could she have gotten here? Had she come to find him?

His view lowered to the water surface sparkling in the glow. As to why, he couldn't be sure, but the level rose once more, but there was no splash from more of it. Hands, fingers, edged across his skin. The gentle touch upon aching shoulders served to release the tension stored up in muscles for many months. Drops splashing onto the water followed by more sheets of relief pouring across his chest, his neck. Fingers rubbed into the aches he could never reach.

He inhaled again. The air revived his consciousness for only a moment. She was behind him. Vivien, the angel he'd come so far to see. He wanted to turn and to view her once more in her bare form, as he had before. He needed to speak to her, but what could he say?

All the many miles he traveled just for this

chance. He hadn't the strength nor courage to rise from the water and face her. Her caress on his body would have to suffice.

The rhythmic motion of her hands along his sides and back told him how much she cared for him. How much she loved him. Doubt surfaced in his mind as to the likelihood of her presence, but he dismissed it. Only one so caring could be so gentle.

Gradually he leaned back, with only a minor grip to the sturdy wooden sides in his palms. His back lay against her soft front. He closed his eyes, relaxed to the bounds of her arms around him. Drops spilt onto his face. His jaw fell ajar, drinking in the spray like under a waterfall.

He could breathe now. He could breathe without pain. Even a deep breath only held a hint of ache to his ribs. Fewer and shorter breaths sent tingles through his nerves, allowing his mind to ease. His head the weight of an anvil, he relaxed the muscles in his neck. Wrapped in the confines of her safe embrace, the concerns for the surroundings slowly faded. The edge he'd always kept wasn't necessary. He was protected. Further inside the sanctuary he sank.

Upon entry into the parlor, decorum required the removal of all hats. As Chester did so, he scanned about the large room. Noticing the elite of the city all sitting within a single room was remarkable. All the political disputes were less important than a fine glass of sherry and a good cigar.

While searching through the room, it took only moments for him to find the Swiss gentleman. He threaded his way through the throng watching the table game. A bit of force was necessary to get to the side of the man. It was a risk coming so near the play, but time wasn't a luxury he had.

As subtly as he could, he moved an open chair close to the table. Just behind the man he sought, he watched a few plays as a dealer dealt a pair of hands. The Swiss gentleman sat on the side of the bank. The opponent seemed content to wager on the player. The stack of chips in front of that one showed he was someone with a lot of money; likely inherited, not bequeathed the sense it took to amass that type of fortune. With the hand going to that player, now appeared a favorable moment to begin the business for which he came.

"I see you haven't lost your nerve?"

Without turning, the man addressed him while keeping his eyes firmly on the new hand of cards. "Nor my skill. What is the reason for this insult?"

"My regrets for the intrusion, but my employer is in urgent need of your service."

The dealer dealt the cards, and this time the wealthy player won the hand.

"You have already cost me money. I remember we have had this conversation before, yes? And when I gave my price, your employer thought me too high. So, why does he send you again?"

Chester knew he would receive this attitude. The answer had to be swift and sure or any chance of success would be lost. This man's reputation for impatience was matched only by his efficiency. "Things have changed."

"For the worst, no doubt, yes?"

Chester paused at the arrogance. "You must know that things aren't as they should be. That is why I am here. To see they are put back on course."

The hand went to the Swiss man's opponent.

Another bet was put on the bank. "And you must know that I am not without my standards for such a situation."

Chester wanted to make the deal in more discreet surroundings. However, he knew as long as there were a substantial amount of chips in front of both of the men at the table, there wasn't a possibility of one of them leaving. Part of the play of the game was the show of no fear. It was a contest which could rage all night, but only one would leave with all the chips of the other.

Slowly, he placed his hand inside his coat. The envelope had been packed with the appropriate amount. As carefully as possible, he slipped the envelope inside the wide pocket of his prospective contractor. The package was noticed. A delicate touch opened the flap and a thumb ran across the top of the bills.

"Is it all there?"

The player won once more.

"We trust the fee is satisfactory," Chester murmured.

"It better be," came the ominous answer. "They must have been more trouble than expected."

A healthy bet was put on the bank.

"Not they. Only one. And he's not one of them."

The bank won the hand. The amount wagered doubled.

"One? How could this be? All those you acquired, and there's one?

Chester took a deep breath. The embarrassment had to be endured. "A man used to killing. They're after him now."

The player won the hand. The wager was again doubled on the bank.

"I only travel alone. You know that."

Chester nodded, although he knew it was un-
seen, or so he thought. "Two have already been removed tonight. The rest are up to you. It is no
matter for us."

The player won the hand again. A sly grin grew
on the opponent's face. A dangerous gesture toward
someone so skilled at taking lives, especially those
for whom he held a grudge. Yet, one who also knew
there would always be an opportunity. That sly grin
may never be forgotten. Not for years.

Chester exhaled with some relief. "We should
hear from you in a week." He rose from his chair.
As he had entered, it took him time to make his way
to the exit. As he turned his back to go through the
door, a gasp rose from the mass. Chester turned
quickly. The game had concluded. A far peek showed
the stack in front of the Swiss gentleman gone. Perhaps an omen for events yet to unfold? On the other
hand, it could be a stroke of luck. Just proper incen-
tive to accept payment and get the job done as soon
as possible.

CHAPTER ELEVEN

A dry throat opened his eyes—thirst brought him out of the daze. A canvas tent was above him. It was the inside of a tent. He rolled onto an elbow. It was his bedroll, but not his tent. He didn't own a tent. Inside the same tent sat a smoldering fire beneath a pot over a spit. Where was he?

The memory from the previous night didn't come to him. He tried to rise, but the ache to his belly kept him on the bedroll. He laid back and tried to remember. The vision of the green salt pork was first into his mind. Then the old barkeep. The search for the Chinese girl was next. Where was the Chinese girl?

The question pulled him out of the bedroll despite the pain. It was then he realized he hadn't any clothes on. The notion that he lost the clothes during the night was worse than the fear of losing the girl. A quick scan about the tent saw her crumpled white clothes. They'd taken her. Those miners came back during the night and took her. The idea couldn't appear more true. When he got to his feet, he cautiously poked his head out of the tent and into the bright sunlight. By the angle of the sun, the morning was half over.

"Good morning to you, sleepyhead. Feeling better?"

To the left he saw three men standing near the tent. "Who are you? Where is this?"

"Name's Jacob McMannus. You're in California."

The answer told him nothing. "I know I am in California. Where are the miners? The miners that took the girl."

"Well," said the bushy-bearded big fellow. "If it's miners you're looking for, they're probably near Cotter. That's maybe ten miles over these hills. More like fifty over flat ground. By the looks of your horse, you were riding him solid for two days."

Cole shook his head. "That don't make sense." The more important matter came back to him. "Where's the Chinese girl?" As the men stood, they looked to each other, then all of them took a step back. In oversized trousers with slacked suspenders, the girl, now with braided hair, stood revealed. It was if he wasn't looking at the same person.

"We loaned her the use of the clothes. Not that we need them back. The man who owned them had a spare. And, well, we didn't want her around the camp in that rag she was wearing. Won't get much done with a female showing skin. She don't talk much English, but she seemed to understand."

Curious to learn other matters, the bent-over stance sent his head in a daze. He grasped the canvas for balance, but his misstep was noticed.

"Looks like you need a bit more rest, son."

Cole nodded, still unaware of the whereabouts of

his clothes and his weapons. He signaled for the girl to come to him. As she did, the men began lifting iron and leather equipment. McMannus came closer.

"We've got the second shift today. Won't likely be back until just before sundown. If you feel the need to stay, we won't mind. I know how it is when you're sick. Don't have much food, though. I'm afraid you'll have to scrape up whatever you can." He turned to catch the other two men. "Get some rest, son. Hope you feel better."

Cole watched him walk away, then looked at the girl. She approached, and he signaled her to come into the tent. About the time she came inside, he retreated to the bedroll. Lifting it in front of him, he again suffered from dizziness. "Where's my clothes?" She stared at him in confusion. "My clothes, dammit. Where are they? And my sidearm—where'd you take them? Did you give it to them? That's why they gave you them clothes?" He finished berating her by pointing his finger with one hand while holding up the bedroll with the other.

She looked to her front with a concerned face, her brow furrowed, searching the checkered flannel. Cole saw that she thought something was wrong with the shirt, rather than realizing that she'd done something wrong.

"Not that. Where are my clothes?" He pointed at his own chest. Her brow eased. She left the tent. In one moment, he thought she understood, but in the next feared she'd run off. He'd just yelled at her. Would he have stayed? He went to the front of the tent, but the steps loosened his balance again. He hadn't been this weak since he nearly starved in the Rocky mountains two years past.

With a grip on the tent he poked his head out

again. He saw her return with both his dark green
shirt and pale trousers. It was hard to choose between which was a more amazing sight: the return
of his clothes or the fact she didn't run away.

The chime rang his entry. He walked to the counter.
Nathan Nichols came from the back room. A smile
quickly came across his face. "Ah, nice to see you
again, Mr. Koenig."

"Good morning to you, Mr. Nichols." He came to
the counter.

"By the looks of you, seems you're going hunting
again."

The notice was startling. "And why do you ask
that?"

Nichols blinked several times. "Well, I wasn't
asking, just commenting. Those baggy trousers, that
jacket with all those pockets, that special hat with
the side pinned up, even wearing the leggings. Sure
seems like you going hunting. Matter of fact, I saw a
man wearing something like that the other day.
Only his looked like they were made of some hide."

The reference was amusing, but held no interest.
"Yes, you are right, Mr. Nichols. I am going hunting, as you say. I will need the usual supplies."

Nichols turned about and searched the shelves.
"Thirty-thirty, if I remember. Five boxes will do?"

"Only if I am fortunate. Make it seven. If I have
more after, I will find something else to hunt." He
smiled at his own humor. It took more than a moment for Nichols to do the same.

"What are you hunting?" asked the gunsmith.

"I have learned one of your grizzly bears is up in
the mountains. I haven't killed one of them as yet. I
think I will enjoy doing so."

"Grizzly, huh? Yes, you will probably need plenty of ammunition for that. I've heard it may take ten shots just to bring one down." While the cartridge boxes were inspected, Nichols began slowly shaking his finger. "You know, you're from Europe. I bet you might know." The comment was immediately uninteresting. Little stood more boring than to talk about the old country. However, Nichols continued. "Have you ever heard of a gunmaker by the name of Mouton?"

He stopped counting the shells. At first he cast an eye at the gunsmith, then lifted his head for a full view. "Yes. Yes, I have heard of that name. Belgian. Normally a military supplier. Why do you ask?"

Nichols went to the back room and spoke at the same time. "Well, that fellow with the leggings I mentioned, he was in here just the other day." As he disappeared behind a wall, his voice could still be heard. "And he brought me this," he said, rounding the wall back into view holding a carbine of sleek design. The wood stock had been poorly kept by the look of its dull finish. Nichols held it with the caring hands of a gunsmith, but not of a shooter.

The delight of seeing a well-made weapon brought a small smile. "May I see it?" He took the weapon from Nichols. As first seen, there were indications of rough treatment, subjected to the elements without proper cleaning of the stock and barrel. However, the mechanism appeared to have been cared for by someone who knew the need to keep it clean. The loading slot was an idea heard about but not seen before now. The pump action was a pure European original. The more he inspected it, the more he wanted it.

"Yes, see?" Nichols said, pointing at the top of the lock. "It's stamped by the gunmaker. 'Mouton.' "

He put it to his shoulder, pulled the trigger and pumped the action. It was smooth, barely a motion at all sliding it back and forth. He had to have it. He looked at the muzzle. "Seven millimeter?"

"Why, yes. That's what I found. I had to make the ammunition specially for it."

"How many cartridges have you made so far?" He carefully inspected the condition of the weapon.

"Well, once I measured the bore, I had to find the proper dye to stamp the brass for the proper dimension. Not an easy task if I may admit. Also, the magazines that he brought me were in terrible condition. I had to clean all the sand and dirt, scour the rust from the springs. It was not easy. Then there was the matter of the slug. With the small bore, I had to forge my own mold. I confess I had to sample many different combinations of how may grains of powder for the space afforded. It took quite a time to get just the right mix. I finally found that it took—" he was stopped by an impatient glare.

"Mr. Nichols, my good friend. How many rounds have you been able to make?"

"Right now, I've only been able to turn out a couple of dozen."

It was adequate. He nodded. "Very well. I will take them."

"Take them?" Nichols questioned. After a moment, he grinned from the statement. "Mr. Koenig, I can't let you take that rifle. It belongs to another man."

He turned to face the gunsmith. "And just what did this man say his name was?"

Nichols scratched his head. "Now let me see.

What was his name. You know, I'm not good with names, except yours, of course. See so many people in here." He blinked several more times. "Cole, I think he said. Yes, that's it. Clay Cole. I remember from the double Cs."

"That is my friend."

"Your friend? Really?" Nichols repeated with his nose crinkled from the minor disbelief. "You know him?"

The mention of the hide leggings put a vision of the subject in his mind. "Of course. He is a rather weathered man from years in the West, no?"

Nichols bobbed his head to one side. "Yes, that looks like him. How do you know him?"

It was better not to look the gunsmith in the eye. He resumed inspecting the carbine. "I met him years ago. I also saw him just recently when he was in San Francisco. I believe he left town, yes?"

"Yes, he did. He said he was traveling up into the Sierras."

"Ah, yes," he said with a wink. "I also remember him telling me that. Yes, it was just the other day that I saw him. He was going hunting, as I am. When he said that, I had some urgent business to attend. Now, I am able to join him. I can take him this weapon. I am sure he will need it where he has gone."

"And how do you know exactly where he has gone?"

It was time to use all his advantage. "Mr. Nichols, my good friend, I am a man who knows the habits of other men. I know my good friend Clay Cole would seek the same as I. When he learns of the bear in his area, it will be natural for him to hunt it. But, as you say, he will need the proper weapon to kill it, no? What did he take with him on his journey?"

Nichols appeared confused. It took him a moment to think of the answer. "Well, I gave him the loan of a Winchester repeater. He took several boxes of forty-five cartridges."

It was the answer best to use. "You see? A good weapon for close-in battles, but not one for hunting just such an animal as a grizzly bear. The small cartridge does not carry enough powder and cannot penetrate the thick skin of the predator." He knew the gunsmith had to agree. The point needed to convince. He lifted the Mouton rifle to show its broad side. "This is the weapon needed. With the shells you have made for it, it will penetrate the bear's thick skin and put the animal down with one well-placed shot." He tucked it under his arm, a posture meant to reinforce the stance that he planned to leave with the Mouton. A moment's hesitation by the gunsmith showed he needed more convincing. "My friend, do not trouble yourself with worry. You know me. I have come here for years and you have all my business. I trust you to make for me the finest ammunition to make my hunts successful. And you have always done fine work. And I have always been pleased with your work. Cannot I ask you to trust me in the same way? I am telling you the truth. I will use this gun only to protect myself and will deliver it to Clay Cole when I find him. You should rest easy, my friend. When I see Clay Cole, he will know that I have his weapon. I will make sure of it."

The sun sank below the crest of the far mountains. Cole sat near the fire. The China girl stirred her brew. He watched her while darting his eyes outside the tent, and inhaled deeply, sensing the fine feeling that he was regaining his strength. It had been many years since he was allowed to sleep most of the day away.

She took a bowl and dipped it into the pot. When she presented it to him, at first he arched away. She held it under his nose, but when he resisted she pushed it to his lips. He slurped the broth rather than drown in it.

The taste was almost like what he imagined grass. The color sure seemed the same. As he swallowed, the slight burn from the heat soon turned to a substance that felt like wax. He waggled his tongue like a horse trying to spit the bit. His motion made her giggle.

"You think that's funny? I don't see you drinking this. What's in it?"

She didn't respond. Instead she slurped some for herself from the same bowl, offering the rest to him. When he didn't accept, she peeked at the bowl, then at him.

"Please."

He widened his eyes at the word. "You can talk?" She didn't reply, but pushed the bowl again at his face. He put his hand on the bowl. "Wait. You can talk? Why didn't you say anything before?" She pushed it at him again.

"Please."

The more he pushed at the bowl, the more she did. Finally, he surrendered and took in the rest of the bowl with her tipping it to his mouth. Once all in, he swallowed. All at once, the grassy taste filled every space. It made him blink several times. When

able to focus, he saw her dip the bowl into the pot
again.

"No more. I'm feeling a heap better now." His answer didn't stop her. Like before, she presented it.
"No. I can't take any more."

"Please."

"No, I said." When she dipped her eyes down, he
guessed he'd finally gotten through to her. She
placed it on the ground in front of him. She rose and
went to the bedroll. When she knelt and began folding it, he shook his head. "What are you doing
now?"

She only glanced at him. "Please."

"Please? Please what?" She continued with the
folding. "Please what? You don't fold it. You roll it.
That's why it's called a bed*roll.*" He tone stopped
her for a moment. Her eyes looked into his. Then he
saw her smile.

"Please."

He shook her head. "Please? Is that all you can
say?"

Her smile shrank. She looked at him as in confusion. "Please?"

He shook his head and looked outside. Just when
he thought he could talk to her. To ask her questions
about herself. "It is all you can say?"

While looking outside, he saw the men from
the morning return. Anxious to have some news,
he rose from the ground and left the tent. He approached McMannus. "Never did have a fair chance
to thank you fellows proper." He held out his hand.
The large, bearded man accepted it graciously. "My
name's Clay Cole. I'm beholden to you for your
kindness."

"No need to thank us," he said, setting down a

thick leather belt with metal hooks. "Was only being neighborly. Like I said, you live out here long enough, you find yourself in a fix just as you were. We was just repaying the same given me by others."

Cole nodded with a grin. "Well, I guess I'm beholden to them and you."

As the man laid down other equipment, he pointed to the tent. Cole followed the direction, looking over his shoulder. In the dimming light, he saw the girl's silhouette through the canvas. "If you ask me," McMannus continued. "You ought to be thanking her. She's the one that got what was in you out of you. It wasn't our doing. All we did is let you two sleep in the wash tent.

The comment brought vague memories of the night before. Flashes of visions flew through his head. The glow, the figure in front of him, the bath. He looked back and forth from the bearded man to the tent. "She was sleeping with me?" he asked in a soft voice. The delusions which swam in his head now came clear. "She was the one."

"What's that you're saying?"

He cleared his head of the vision. He took more notice of the equipment. "What line you fellows in?"

"We're loggers."

Not until it was said did he even notice the tall, broad-trunked trees surrounding them. A scan about showed acres of trees. "Don't know if I ever been around the type of work you're doing."

"Ah, no matter." McMannus looked to Cole. "By the looks of you, you're used to prairie grass."

Cole peeked at his clothes. Despite the urge to complain that he'd seen many a hill, some with snow along with the sands found in the deserts of Texas and New Mexico, he did fit the look of a man who worked the plains. "I guess you could say that."

It wasn't long before the day came to an end and campfires provided the only light. A meal of pan-fried cornmeal with bacon mixed in served as the evening meal. Cole was a bit shy at first to be putting any more pig in his stomach, but the smell of grease bubbling was too much to resist.

They all huddled next to the fire. The night brought a cool breeze from the west. Cole looked to the moon, where clouds traveled in front of its glow. "Might be a storm coming."

"Nah," McMannus said, looking up. "It's just the way these mountains are. Not much to compare it to."

Cole nodded. "I hear that. I rode through some fog for a few nights."

The logger shook his head along with the rest of his friends. "Rare that happens up here. Sometimes, though. You must have been near the sea. Rolls in almost every night during the summer. But the air dries out usually before it gets up here."

The mention of the sea brought to mind the big city and just how far he stood from where he'd come from, and from what or whom he wanted. "Reckon how far San Francisco is from here?"

"Probably forty or more miles from the bay. Maybe near sixty. I can't ever keep track as much as we're moving."

"Moving?" The mention was peculiar. "Moving to where?"

McMannus chuckled, as did his friends. "Moving to new ranges." Cole's wondrous gaze about was noticed. "Can't cut down every tree you see, son. Most of these are too small."

"Small?"

"Yes, small. Probably burned at one time. Maybe twenty, thirty years ago. Probably from lightning. Anyway, these trees will be ready in another ten years or so. No, what we cut down are the really big trees. Spruce, pine and the real whoppers, the sequoia. Most over two hundred years old. The truly big ones are three hundred, three hundred and fifty feet high with a thirty-foot diameter at the base." The other loggers concurred.

Cole accepted it all as truth. An owl's hoot brought him from imagining their descriptions. "So, where are you headed?"

"Wherever the company sends us," said McMannus.

"I heard the foreman say we might be heading back to the west," spoke another logger of younger years. Peculiar looks from his friends made him defend the comment. "The talk is there's twenty thousand acres ready for use."

"Where?" questioned the booming voice of McMannus.

"About fifty miles to the northwest," was the answer.

The large and older McMannus shook his head. "No. That can't be right. No one owns that land except the state. There's still miners in those hills working claims," he said with a chuckle. Cole shot his glance at the China girl. The chuckle stopped. "But, if you're right, could make some money. There is some old trees there."

A queasy feeling came over Cole, but it wasn't from the bacon. All the killing he'd seen wasn't from one people's hatred for another. All wars are based on money. Of the wars he'd seen and fought, they were almost always over money. Whether to work the soil or dig it up for gold, it was always first needed to rid it of the people living on it.

"I'm going to grab some sack," said the young logger. "We work the first shift tomorrow."

"I'll be right behind you," McMannus said as the others left. Cole moved closer to the big man.

"What do you think would need to happen to them miners working those claims?"

McMannus shrugged. "I guess they get paid off or run off by the law."

The answer was the same one for the next question on his tongue. If the law wasn't involved as yet, then as the dapper man in the hotel said, it would be up to the law of the gun. He didn't want to bother his new friend by asking. He turned instead to the tent. The girl's silhouette still rose and sank through the canvas. The silence allowed McMannus to view as well.

"Where did you get her?" he asked.

Cole shrugged. "I was helping some folks. Chinamen in those hills you mentioned. They said she wasn't wanted by the others in the camp. So, rather than make her stay where she wasn't wanted, I thought I could set her off somewhere she would be."

McMannus nodded at the ground. "A concubine?"

"That's what they called her. I guess that's like a whore. It was the way they called them in Wyoming."

"Yes, and in other places. Seems the Orientals are just about everywhere now. The foreman, he runs them off before they open up any opium dens. Seen that before in other camps, and if a man smokes the pipe, he isn't good for the others working around him. Could get someone killed."

It was a familiar story. The same had been said

about every profession that had to deal with the lure of the drug. As Cole considered the fate of Ho Yung and the rest of those prospectors, McMannus spoke again.

"She was probably sold. Sold by someone she knew. An uncle, maybe a father."

"Sold? You mean like a slave?"

"That's what they are. A female to a family that's starving is worth more in money than what work she can do. You know, what you should do, a fellow like yourself, is head to Arizona. I heard there's nothing but space there, and the Orientals there keep good standing with the whites there. Take her there."

Cole cocked his head to one side. "I don't know about Arizona. Seems a long way away."

"Well, you may be right. I just thought a man such as yourself would do better there than here in California. Here the place is filling up fast." McMannus smacked Cole's thigh. "Son, I'll be getting to bed. Nice talking with you."

As he rose, Cole looked to the friendly logger. "I thank you again for your kindness. I'll be setting out in the morning." They shook hands. As McMannus disappeared into the darkness, Cole turned his view to the tent. If he planned on leaving in the morning, sleep was needed.

He went into the tent. She had already spread the bedroll. He didn't know if he cared for all her attention. There wasn't any room in his life to be dragging around a girl, much less one that didn't know how to speak English. However, the more he stood, the weaker his head. He didn't have the fight in him to explain it wasn't proper to be sleeping in the same bedroll. "Only sleep," he said, waving his hands.

Slowly, he settled next to her. She gave him most of the space. He rolled onto his side, his conscience bothering him over his treatment of her. Although he couldn't bring himself to apologize, he thought he could end the day with good manners. "Get some sleep, Lulu."

She answered the only way she knew. "Please."

CHAPTER TWELVE

Hunger drove them down the mountain. When they got to the valley, the best place in view was the food shack. While the others headed to take their relief of nature in the latrines from the overnight trip, he wanted to get some food. The step into the door showed the place as he remembered it. The long single table in the center was still there. So was the bar. So was Henry Cooper. "What do you say, you old bastard?"

The skinny old man with the patchy beard looked back over his shoulder. His surprise was seen by his four-tooth smile. "Will Hayward. Haven't seen you in six months if it was a day. Come in here. Where have you been?"

He walked to the bar. "Been laid up." As he came close to the man at the bar, he eased his right arm up in a weak motion to accept the old man's handshake. The effort was noticed.

"What's this?" asked Henry Cooper, pointing at the arm. "You get hurt in the mine?"

The story had been told every day since it

happened. "Oh, I got attacked by this drifter two
months ago. A fellow came into Sweaty Hal's place.
I was minding my own business when he threw a
knife at me. Damn near bled to death." As his
friends came into the bar, Henry greeted them, shaking their hands as they passed by and took places at
the long table.

Henry brought over bowls to the table and placed
them in front of them. He spoke to Will Hayward
while doling out heapings. "Just up and attacked
you, huh? What did this fellow look like?"

That memory was etched into his mind. "Tall.
Seemed like a stout fellow, although he had a coat
on. Sometimes that hides a man's shape. Mean, too.
As mean as I ever seen a man. Likely a killer on the
run. We were just enjoying ourselves. It was payday
and we needed to drink off some aches." He shook
his head. "But he came in and made it plain that he
was there for everybody to listen to. You know
Sweaty Hal, don't you, Henry?"

"Oh yeah, I know him."

"Well, Old Hal tried to get him out of there. Fellow was looking for a woman. Probably his wife
that run off from him. Couldn't blame her a bit after
seeing that fellow. He'll likely kill her if he ever
finds her." He looked at the jugs stacked on the
shelves behind the bar. "Get over here and pour me
a drink, you old buzzard. Can't lift a jug no more
with this arm."

Henry came around the long wood plank, took a
jug, pulled the cork and poured the liquor into a
glass. "Tall man you said he was?" Will nodded
as he slurped the whiskey. "Kind of mean, too?"
Again, Will nodded, finishing the glass, then point-

ing for it to be refilled. Henry did so while still talking. "Black wide-brimmed hat? Pistol on the hip? Had a Oriental woman with him?"

The question seemed odd. Will nodded. "Yeah, that's what he looked like. Don't know anything about no woman though, Oriental or not. Why are you asking, Henry?"

The slim old man poured himself a drink and leaned an elbow on the plank. "There's a man in here two days ago looked just like that."

About to drink, Will slowly lowered the glass from his lips. "What did you say?" Will glanced behind and saw his friends had also heard the news.

"I'm telling you the truth. A man fitting the description stood in the very place as you. Came in here looking like he'd been riding a long time. Like you said, like he'd been on the run. Just like an outlaw. So, he comes in here, starts talking about how he hates people like you and me. How the Orientals are better, and how he wished they'd take over the country. And they will, too, if we don't ship them all back to their own country."

Will looked to his friends. The rage returned. He slapped the glass on the plank. "Are you saying that the man that tried to kill me was just in here?"

"Yes," the old man said. "That's what I'm telling you. And do you know what he did that day? He damn near killed Stu and Farmer when they were in here. That Oriental girl I told you about, she was inviting them to have a poke at her, and they was takers. You know, it'd been a long time." The old man threw the shot down his throat. "Can't blame a man for wanting a poke now and then."

"So, what did he do? The man you talked about?"

asked Will, not interested in the woman so much as
the man that put a knife in him.

"Well, the next thing I knew, he was, that fellow,
was walking out of here. He'd ate my food and didn't
bother paying me a nickel for it. I rounded a few of
the fellows around here, not wanting to get killed
by this stranger. When we caught up with them,
they were back by the latrines. That woman was
selling pokes, and this fellow, maybe her pimp, he
smashed both Farmer and Stu with a shovel. Probably 'cause he wasn't getting his cut of the deal.
Damned near killed them. Either way, they ain't
been back to work and they ain't getting paid. Take
away a man's way of making a living and it's like
near killing him."

Will eye's widened, his breath growing shorter
the more he listened. He raised his right arm.
"You're telling me. I can't lift a shovel or pick since.
Only because of some of the men have I been able to
eat," he said, pointing at his glass for Henry Cooper
to refill. Once the glass was full, Will picked it up.
"A man gots to drink, too."

"Hell, yes," Henry said, refilling Will's and his
own glasses. Will threw his down quickly.

"So, which way did this outlaw go?"

Refreshed from the two nights of rest, Cole set out
at dawn with the girl. He followed a mountain trail
through the towering redwoods. An occasional
peek up made them appear to be the pillars sup-
porting the sky. Sunlight filtered between the broad
long limbs, leaving a web of shadows on the ground.

During a long climb up a considerable grade, he
felt the palomino needed a rest and some water. He
held the girl's arm as she jumped from the rump,

then he slid from the saddle. He took the canteen, cupped his hand and allowed the horse a drink. While doing so, he scanned about. The numerous trees numbered in amounts he didn't know how to count. The pretty scene was matched by the near dead silence. Only occasional calls from curious birds echoed through the woods.

He glanced over his shoulder. The girl used the time to search for whatever herbs or mushrooms found under the growth on the ground in the near constant shade. As he watched her, his mind turned to the problem facing him. Where would she belong?

He poured more water in his hand while he again looked about. The beauty of the forest also clouded any sense of direction and made any attempt to search for another settlement very difficult. He took a sip of his own, then huffed out a breath of frustration. This isn't how he planned his new life in California.

The attitude of the locals didn't cotton to these foreigners with different faces. Although he had witnessed the conflicts of cultures firsthand, whether with these people or the native tribes, there was always a group to collect those that had been scattered. The different tribes also had their own cruel treatment for others of competing nations. It wasn't uncommon for a Kiowa to be a captive or tortured by the Pawnee. As he looked to the girl, the same idea came to him about her. Despite her soiled past with men she wasn't married to, she might have come from a different tribe of her own. One which didn't fit with the rest. The notion only served to burden his mind. He had no idea to which tribe she belonged.

Satisfied the palomino had taken its fill, he took a

few more for himself and went to her. She moved
along the ground, waddling and settling, picking
between the leaves and small ferns, collecting bits
and pieces of some growth she apparently saw
as food.

"Thirsty?"

His question startled her. After she saw the offer
of the canteen, she put her collection into the vest
pocket of the flannel shirt. The suggestion won over
her desire for more searching. She took the canteen
and sipped. Cole's curiosity forced him to tug
open her pocket with a finger and peek. Her eyes
widened with his action.

"Food?" he inquired, seeing little more than
twigs and a few green globs. He pointed at the
pocket. "Food?" Since she didn't show any understanding, he pointed fingers at his open mouth.

She arched a brow at his strange motion, then
shook her head. Her spoken reply was of no use for
him, so he shrugged. When she nodded, she dipped
her eyes and rubbed along her sleeve. After a few
strokes, he realized it was meant as some kind of
salve.

"Oh," he said. "Medicine." She leaned and angled her ear to him. "Medicine?" He rubbed his
own sleeve. "For when you're hurt. Itch."

"It-ch," she stammered.

Cole nodded. "Yes. Itch. That's right. Good."

She looked at him with an odd face. "Itch." She
rubbed her arm "Itch, good. Itch good."

Cole shook his head. "No. Itch not good. Itch is
bad." He rubbed his arm and so did she. "Itch bad."

She mimicked his motion. "It-ch bad." She patted
her arm. "Bad."

He nodded until he thought what she might

mean. "Itch bad, but your arm is not bad. That is your arm. Not bad. Arm. Arm is good."

"Arm." She patted her own limb. "Arm good."

He nodded and smiled at his success to teach her a word. "That's right. Arm good. Itch bad." Despite his success at making her repeat the words, the girl's brow recessed in a manner of confusion. So much so, he wasn't confident she really understood. Feeling the need to take matters in hand and demonstrate what he meant, he leaned closer to take her and reached for her arm.

A blast rippled through the air. Tree bark splintered about.

Reflex forced Cole to lunge behind cover. He pushed the girl's shoulders, knocking her onto the ground.

CHAPTER THIRTEEN

The Colt was in his right hand in an instant. Rolling to his side, the shooter came from the trees to gain a clear angle. Cole cocked and fired. The bullet went high. The shooter knelt. The shape of a Springfield carbine was recognizable, but the face wasn't. A broad hat cast it in shadow. The shooter levered another round in the chamber. Cole pulled back the hammer and fired. The shooter shot. The bullet popped leaves and dust in the air.

While the shooter levered, Cole pulled the hammer and fired once more, then reaction took over, fanning his palm against the hammer, sending as much lead at the shooter as possible. Thick smoke clouded the view. Once it thinned, the shooter lay on his back in the bright sunshine. Cole propped himself on an elbow to get a look at the face.

Another shot rang out. Sensing the direction, he faced to the left. A plume of smoke came through the trees. Cole aimed and cocked the hammer. The pin fell on an empty cartridge.

He fell on his back and with elbows and heels

crawled backward behind a wide tree trunk. He glanced up and behind. The girl hugged her knees to her chest as she leaned against another trunk. He couldn't speak to her. A single palm pushed in her direction would have to do as the order to stay put.

As quickly as possible, he opened the chamber-gate and rolled the cylinder to empty the spent rounds. Only able to get three cartridges with his right hand from the belt loops, he slid three fresh loads into the cylinder and snapped the chamber-gate closed with his thumb. Back with his finger on the trigger, he cocked the hammer and edged his head around the trunk.

A bullet sprayed tree bark into his face and mouth. He spat them out. "That you, Charlie?" he yelled, hoping for a reply so to locate his attackers. He looked right at the palomino, which strayed further down the path from the gunfire. He had to get to the Winchester in the scabbard. "Can you hear me, Charlie? Looks like Malachi won't be with you no longer. Might want to think about leaving before you join him." The attempt to goad a response had no effect.

Cole edged back farther behind the tree so as to get on one knee and scan about for the rest. He looked to the body on the path. There was no clear line of sight to come from there. He knew Charlie or one of the bunch lay in wait to the left. A bend in the path kept him guessing if more fire would come his way from further uphill, or if they'd double back behind him. The more choices he thought they had, the less he possessed to counter.

As he gauged the distance to the bend, footsteps erupted at his back. He turned, Colt in front, finger wrapped around the trigger. The girl stood behind him. Behind her stood Tom Perkins with a rifle at his shoulder.

"Move!"

The girl stood firm. In one instant he prepared to see her gut blown through. The next instant he chose to see her live. He aimed and fired. The bullet flew over her shoulder and into Tom's chest. The gun jolted from impact, but did not drop from Tom's hand.

Cole waved for her to move. The signal was enough to get her from the line of fire. Tom stood, staggered. Blood filled his shirt. Cole cocked the pistol and aimed at arm's length. The crack of rifle fire drew his attention back to the bend in the path. Only the maze of broad trees kept him from being a clear target.

He ducked behind the trunk. He glanced to aim at Tom, but the wounded man was now out of sight. If he poked his head out from either side he risked it getting blown from his shoulders. Once more, he looked to the palomino. Then he eyed the girl.

At a crouch, he darted to where she hid against another redwood. He knelt by her side. If the idea on his mind was to work, she'd have to do her part. Despite his knowledge of her lack of English, he had to speak it out for even himself to understand.

"I need you take the pistol," he said while taking the remaining three cartridges from the loops, ejecting the spent shell, then loading the new rounds. "Point and fire. Don't matter if you hit nothing, just make them think I'm here." He pointed at the pistol. "Five shots is all you got. Don't fire them all at once. Just one every three seconds or so."

He got off of the knee and squatted. "I'm going to

make a run for the horse." He bobbed his head in the direction of the palomino. The girl's eyes widened. Her jaw quivered. He had to make her not only understand, but fire the pistol as he wanted.

He tried pushing the weapon into her hand, but she yanked her hand away. "Take it!" He jabbed his finger on the barrel. "Shoot the gun or we die." He pointed again at the palomino. "I'm running after the rifle on the horse." With her face still twisted in knots, he formed his hand like a gun and tucked it next to his shoulder. "I'm getting the rifle off the horse." He pointed at the palomino. The girl also glanced at the palomino.

Like a shot from a cannon, she jumped to her feet and ran to the palomino.

"Where you going?"

Over open ground she ran directly to the horse. Any second she'd be cut down by a volley of fire. Cole ran into the open himself to draw fire. He fired at the direction of the bend in the path. A single shot and a plume came out of the woods. Bark popped into the air. More shots ripped through the woods. Limbs, leaves and branches flew all around him. He cocked and fired at the plume, but the shadows kept any attacker from view.

A shot came from the left. Cole twisted at the hip, bringing the Colt to aim at the first motion he saw. Tom knelt, one hand holding and aiming the rifle, the other clutched against his bleeding chest. Cole thumbed the hammer and squeezed the trigger. The bullet went through the cheek and out of the back of Tom's head. The body slumped in a heap. Now he had a rifle, but it was closer to the path and would cost a lot of lead coming his way. He glanced back at the girl.

She'd made it to the horse without a scratch. With a snatch on the reins, she steadied the palomino like a wrangler, then drew the Winchester. Cole blinked twice just to be sure what he was seeing. A smile creased his face.

A bullet popped dirt at her feet. Cole fired at the bend, cocked the hammer and fired once more. He looked behind. She ran with the rifle in her hands. The whir of a slug passed by his head. Reflex made him raise the Colt, cock the hammer and pull the trigger. A loud but hollow click is all that followed.

Out of ammunition, he dove behind one of the trunks. Bullets trailing his path shaved the tree of bark. The girl ran to him. If she ran right at him she'd be in the same spot as he was when the bullet missed him.

Cole rose and ran to her. He raised his hands, palms open. The girl tossed the rifle as she ran, then dropped face first. Cole caught the Winchester and levered the action while twisting about. With a curled finger on the bail, he pulled the trigger with each stroke. The rapid fire from the repeater sent slugs into the trees near the bend in the path. With seven shots gone, he went to the girl. His heart stopped, expecting to see a bullet blasted through her. He grabbed the collar of the flannel shirt and dragged her to the nearest tree.

Sure he had momentary cover, he rolled her onto her back. He saw her eyes open and he was certain she was dead, but she blinked. He met her eyes. He sensed a smile on his face, but she still appeared terrified. "It's all right now. You done good."

She nodded at him. "Itch good."

He nodded and smiled. "That's right," he said to her, not wanting to cause her to fret. "Itch good."

A blast turned him back to the bend in the path. The echo was lower and louder. For a moment he recognized the sound, but dismissed the possibility from his mind with the shake of his head. He pointed at the girl. "You stay here." He jabbed the ground with his finger. "Here."

He levered the action and rose at a crouch. He crept to the nearest tree, then the next, and then the next. Another blast rippled through the air. Return fire echoed like that from a Sharps. He went wide to the left, passed Tom Perkin's body and proceeded to flank the fire.

As he went from one spot to the next, he listened for motion among the trees. A rustle brought his attention to the left. He crept along a heading to the north, seeking a better position to locate the source of the gunfire.

His concentration ahead, his foot stumbled over an object. He looked down. A body lay crumpled on the ground with the face stuck in the dirt. He bent to turn the shoulder. It was Charlie Biggersby. Cole stood confused.

A glance back through the trees showed the angle from where he came. Likely the leader had the same thoughts of flanking around the end. However, Cole didn't remember fire coming from this direction. He didn't fire at the spot, either. He bobbed his head to the side and farther to the east he spotted the bend in the path. So who shot Charlie here?

The question wasn't one to ponder at the moment. Omaha Sam was out there somewhere.

CHAPTER FOURTEEN

Gunshots erupted further inside the forest. Cole stepped over Charlie's body and went with the Winchester poised in front. The sound of the shots were between two different shooters and two different rifles. He followed the echoes. The trail took him up steep ground.

He ran around the massive trees. When he lost the direction of the shots, he paused. More gunfire brought a renewed sense of their direction. All the while during the run, he couldn't be sure who was shooting and for what purpose.

A blast from the right put him on his knees from the percussion. The explosion was very near. He proceeded closer, the rifle against his shoulder. He thumbed the hammer back and his finger touched the trigger. When another shot echoed, he recognized the direction. An overhang in the woods was an ideal nest for a shooter. He went wide around it to higher ground so as to see it better. Sneaking around another trunk, he could see the smoke coming from the rifle shots.

Slowly, he crept down the slope. Certain the shooter hid among the thick brush, he charged at the nest. As he neared, the path led him where no trees grew. Movement down and to the right away from the nest caught his eye. Omaha Sam stood in a small depression taking dead aim at him with a rifle. Cole froze. A shot rang out.

Omaha Sam fell backward in a lifeless tumble down the incline. Cole turned back left and poised the Winchester in front of him. A shooter knelt with a bolt-action rifle.

Cole again propped the Winchester against his shoulder.

The shooter turned him, hands high and a smile on his face. "Don't shoot, my friend. I just saved your life."

The greeting didn't sway his aim. "Who are you?" he yelled.

Still with the smile in place, the man stood. "My name is Koenig." A better look at him showed baggy-hipped trousers, a coat with three pockets on each side and tight cloth leggings up to the knee.

Cole kept the Winchester steady. "I'm beholden to you for choosing me over Sam down there. I ain't ungrateful. But why'd you do it?"

The man with the slight cut to his words looked at the body below, shrugged, then looked back at Cole. "I heard the shots and saw them attacking you. It didn't seem fair, the three against one, so I thought you could use the help."

"Get yourself into other people's affairs, do you?" The question posed a problem for himself the instant he asked it. After all, why was he there? Despite the self-questioning, he kept the aim on the stranger.

Another shrug came before the answer. "I do not like to see innocent people hurt."

"Innocent? What makes you think I'm innocent? They may have been the law. I may be an outlaw. How would you know the difference just by listening to gunshots?"

The smile increased as the arms gradually came down. "If you were an outlaw, then you would have shot me by now. Come, my friend. Put down your rifle. Let us rest and enjoy our victory over those men who wanted to harm you. I know you want to rest after such a battle, no?"

Cole's conscience nagged him. All this stranger said turned true, but it was the swagger in the words that bothered him most. Still, when he thought that it could have been him at the bottom of the hill with a bullet in the head, it was at least polite to lower the Winchester. "Can't argue that," he said with a nod.

The stranger came closer, hand extended in a friendly gesture. Cole accepted the handshake. "It is good to be friends now, yes?"

Another point which couldn't be argued. He nodded. "Clay Cole."

The man opened his palm in the direction down the hill. "I have a camp not too far from here. Join me, and we will eat." He turned to pick up his bolt-action rifle. Cole kept his finger ready on the Winchester trigger. He watched as the man casually picked up the weapon.

"If it's all the same to you," he said, raising the Winchester. "I'll take the rifle. It will keep us friends." The man raised his brow, and without much resistance handed over the rifle. Once empty-handed, the man proceeded down the hill.

Cole followed at an angle so he could watch the stranger's hands. As they came across Omaha Sam's body, the stranger slowed his step long enough to admire his shooting. A smug grin grew over his face and he nodded at Cole.

"A good shot, don't you think?"

Cole glanced at the bullet hole in the temple. Taking pride in killing, much less bragging about the shot wasn't in his nature. "Got the job done." The slight soured the smug grin. They went down the hill, angling through the many trees. As they descended, Cole wanted to keep an eye on this fellow, but soon the number of trees between them doubled with each of them taking different paths. "You never said what you were doing out here by yourself." With so many trees passing by view, only peeks of the man could be seen.

"I was hunting the game here. I have heard of a bear being in these woods. I very much want to kill a bear. The grizzly, I've heard it called. I have never seen this grizzly bear. Have you?"

Cole tried to angle closer, but the count of trees increased, leaving little room to change direction and walk between. He bobbed his head, trying to keep sight of the stranger. "Yeah, I have. Mean critter. Some over a thousand pounds and stand twelve feet high. Not an animal I'd be looking to meet up with. Damn near had my arm bit off by one." He raised his voice in an attempt to get an equally loud reply. The stranger's voice turned faint.

"Bit off your arm? How exciting. You see, that is the reason of the hunt. It is the excitement that what you are hunting . . ." The voice faded.

Cole went closer to where he last saw the stranger. He went back up the incline to gain a

better look. Once there, no sign of the man existed.
With two rifles in hand he wouldn't be able to
shoot. He leaned the Winchester against the tree
and opened the bolt action. The chamber was empty.
No ammunition lay below the lock to spring up. He
had taken an empty weapon. A useless weapon,
and the stranger knew it.

Cole dropped the bolt action and snatched the
Winchester. He pulled the hammer back once more,
then scanned left and right. With cautious steps, he
went farther in the direction of the last path of the
stranger. He listened closely for footsteps, the snap
of branches or limbs, the rustling of leaves, anything to give him the direction of the stranger.

Rifle at the ready, he ducked through the low
limbs and went deeper into the woods. The tint of
faded green caught his eye. He approached cautiously, one step after the other, balancing on the
toes so not to displace leaves with his weight.
Through the dense growth he recognized the shape
of the coat.

Would he shoot this man? He'd no reason. This
man saved him from a bullet. Only a gut instinct
gnawing at his insides pushed him not to trust the
foreigner. A squeeze of the trigger was an easy settlement. The stain of a murderer was a bloody hole
in the back. He eased his finger on the trigger.

Through the leaves he came upon the coat. In an
instant he saw its shape strung across two limbs.
His eyes went wide. A familiar ratchet drew his attention behind. The stranger was up the incline
aiming a rifle at Cole. The Mouton rifle.

A loud chuckle pounded the wind. "The prey
may be hunting you."

CHAPTER FIFTEEN

Cole rolled backward, pivoting on his right leg as the shot rang off. Bark and debris showered the air. Once his shoulders hit the ground, he continued the roll under the dense growth. When he butted against a spruce trunk, he sprang to his feet and dodged from sight.

He knew the weapon used against him. It was faster, straighter, and had more power. The slug could pass right through some of these smaller trunks. If he poked his head from the side, he could lose it. If he stayed, it was a short matter of time before he'd be flanked and killed. How this man got his own rifle troubled him. He thought he could measure men, and the gunsmith seemed an honest fellow. Whatever tactic was used couldn't be troubling his mind. Not at this time.

He poked the Winchester around the trunk, fired wildly, levered again and squeezed another round. With that, he levered again but ran to the next tree with a wide trunk and knelt behind it. He edged his eye around the end but saw nothing. If he was to

survive, he'd have to maneuver around enough
cover to get a better angle. He needed some bearing
to know where to go. It was a risk to reveal his own
position, but he had to try. "You with that bunch?
Charlie and them?" The lack of a reply didn't dis-
courage. He scanned behind and to the side. "Figured a fellow such as yourself to be a heap smarter
than to join fellows like that. That why you kill
them for me? Wanted me to yourself? Ambrose
Waterfield must have paid a pile of money for your
kind."

A rustle brought his aim to the right. Without a
target, he held his fire. He'd need every bullet. He
crouched and stepped backward, only glancing behind to sight the best place to stop. As he went the
dense growth above shaded the light. He settled
next to a spruce with low limbs. Rounding the trunk
on his knees, he saw the growth only thickened
further into the forest. The good for him was it left
little room for an attack from that angle. The bad
was it wouldn't provide for further retreat.

As he scanned left and right without a sign of the
man's presence, he lay prone to lessen his chances
of getting hit. As seconds then minutes passed,
his confidence grew, then sagged. The question of
whether to stay or scamper to a better place teased
his mind. He shook the distraction from his head. A
crack of leaves brought his attention to the left. He
eased the Winchester stock under his chin, closed
his left eye and curled his right finger around the
trigger. An ounce more pressure would drop the
hammer.

As the crunch grew louder, he managed the image of a boot through the dangling leaves. If he
raised the rifle for a shot at the chest or head, the

sound surely would attract a barrage of bullets his way. Peeking through the low hanging limbs provided no view for such a shot. The boot came closer. It was now in clear view. It wouldn't be a mortal shot, but it may be the best one he'd get.

He sighted the buckled legging. When it squared in front of the barrel, he fired.

The blast sent smoke all in front, clouding his view. The second after, he saw nothing. Instinct rolled him to the side. A hail of bullets pelted the limbs and trunk of the spruce. Cole returned fire through the leaves. The shot gave away where he was, so he levered and sidestepped left, Winchester at the shoulder, finger on the trigger.

One long swooping limb passed, then another. At the end of the reach of the spruce tree, a narrow space wound to the next. Blood splatter soaked the dirt. He saw the red trail lead further away. To flank the wounded man, he continued to backpedal around the next spruce. Each step was carefully placed to lessen any noise. He watched carefully to see if the stranger would stumble back through the spot he'd been hit. When he cleared the tree, another bare space came into view. Two steps away lay a gully. As he glanced, he saw the man lying in the gully, the Mouton barrel rising in an aim at him.

Cole dove as the shot rang out. When he hit the ground, his finger pulled the trigger, sending a wild shot into the high branches. He rolled to a knee, but more shots at him through the leaves forced him back on elbows and knees, crawling with the rifle cradled in his arms to the next wide trunk.

He watched as best he could for any movement, expecting the wounded man to change positions. The voice startled him. "My friend, are you hurt?"

The direction seemed to come from the same place he last saw the man. Since he knew where the stranger was, there was no need to return the same favor.

He had to get around to the left in order to get a clear shot, but that meant risking bullets coming his way.

"You are a good fighter."

Cole ignored the compliment, but used the sound of the voice to center on the man's location. He looked left and saw a clearing that sloped enough to keep the shooter in view. That was as long as the shooter laid in the gully. Should the man stand to get a better view, then Cole was a dead man. Again, he crawled on knees and elbows to the left.

"This is a magnificent weapon. Where would you get such an elegant rifle here in America?"

To be quiet meant moving slow. Even a rustle of dirt could get him shot. Fearing the crown of his hat might gain notice, he peeled it from his head, letting it fall onto the dirt. Once certain he'd not been detected, he resumed the crawl.

"You know, if circumstances were different, we could become good friends, don't you think? I believe we would have a pleasant time sitting down to dinner and recalling our adventures. I would very much like talking to you."

Cole moved to where the gully angled further down the slope. If he went farther left, he'd have to slide into the gully and risk being seen. Even the slide into the gully might create too much noise and alert the stranger. He carefully peeked behind him. The slope increased down further into dense trees. It could take precious time to attempt to go down the slope in order to cross the gully and not be noticed. He eased breath into his lungs. He'd gone as far as he could.

He thumbed the Winchester hammer back, cautiously rising to a knee. The first view above the gully bank was of the stranger still peering in Cole's former direction. With the Winchester nearly at the shoulder he eased his finger to the trigger.

A shrill echoed through the woods. A woman's panicked cry pulled his attention to the right. A glance back at the stranger showed he'd been seen. The Mouton rifle fired wild. Cole lost balance and pulled the trigger, sending errant lead to the sky and tumbling back. The momentum carried him like a stone down the slope. Bullets popped the dirt around him. Fearing if he stopped rolling, he'd be an easier target, he huddled his shoulders in an effort to escape the barrage.

Soon he found himself unable to stop, due to the momentm gained from the steep angle. The force of the roll tore the Winchester from his hands and lifted him off the ground, landing with a bounce on his hips. He reached in an attempt to grab any of the trees or surrounding brush—anything to slow him down. His head struck the hard dirt, sending him into a daze.

From above, he sighted the stranger hobbling one tree at a time and trying to aim the Mouton, but no shots came his way. The jolts to his body pushed the wind from his chest. Only through a last effort did he snag a bush to slow his momentum. Once at a stop, he dared not release the bush. A peek behind showed the end of the slope was a cliff. No telling what was below, but if he let go of the small twigs wrapped through his fingers he'd find out the sure way.

Footsteps stirred his dizzy mind back to the slope. The smug chuckle filled his ears, but his sight was blurred from the knock on the head. The stranger came at him with the Mouton poised on the hip to shoot.

"I told you we would get a chance to talk."

Cole blinked, trying to see him clearly. Without a weapon of any kind, it was his only chance to stall the stranger from shooting. Besides that one tactic, he had no others. "What do you want to say? How you can make a perfect shot from five feet away?"

The remark increased the chuckle. "No. That is not what I wanted to talk about. I just wanted to say that I think you are a good man. Not like the others. Yes, you are who I expected."

As the stranger raised the Mouton to square with Cole's eyes, a notion came to mind. "That's why you killed Charlie and the others? You thought they were me?"

It was enough to get the stranger to pause his aim. "In part, yes, that is true. But there is the other reason. A more important reason."

"What important reason?"

The stranger lowered his aim. "Why, the important reason of money, of course."

"Money? Waterfield paid you to kill those men, too?"

The stranger shook his head. "He did not pay me to kill them. No, that is not what I meant. He paid me to keep them from taking what he has."

"Don't make sense," Cole said, in a try to keep the man from shooting. His vision was clearing and he could see the muzzle dance and sway from his direction. If he were to rush the stranger, the odds were still good he'd be shot dead before he could get to his feet. With the stranger propped against a tree up the slope, even the climb would take precious seconds. He had to stall, but had little to use as reasons. "What does Waterfield have that they could take?"

Another chuckle came from that smug grin. "Let us say more than you could imagine. Someone as yourself is just the type of man he wanted." The stranger again raised the rifle.

"What makes you think he wouldn't want *you* dead?"

The aiming of the rifle didn't pause. "Because who would he get to do it?"

Cole winced as he saw the barrel come level with his own eyes. "Why not that Chester fellow?"

"I have thought of that. I will deal with him when the ferry comes for me in two days."

Something had to be said or done. The instant thought of throwing dirt at the shooter came to mind, but the distance was too far to even make it up the slope. Besides, just risking his grasp on the bush might send him over the cliff. Cole looked at the muzzle, took a deep breath, and decided this was the end. "I could use that dinner you promised."

The stranger grinned at the remark. "I will have it alone in your honor."

Cole closed his eyes.

Vibration jostled his body. He heard no shot, but knew the sound never came with the slug. His body swayed left, then right. The ground itself was moving. Confused, he opened his eyes. The stranger was thrown to the side and dropped the rifle.

Like on a bucking horse, Cole tightened his grip

on the bush and tried to focus, but his vision was blurred by the violent shake.

The stranger stumbled forward and waved his hands back to retain his stance, but without the tree to steady his balance he kept stepping in a clumsy manner directly toward the cliff. In a second, he took two steps and not a third. The curled-brim hat flew from view, as did its owner.

Faint cries of terror echoed off the canyon walls. As soon as they faded, the shaking stopped.

Cole lay on his back. He stared at the blue sky. Never one to pay much mind to help from the heavens, he now had to consider there just might be something to the habit of prayer.

He sucked wind into his lungs. In disbelief, he carefully pulled himself upright and on hands and knees got to the tree that the stranger had leaned against. Once he was on sure footing, he stood and picked up his Mouton rifle, still in a bit of a daze from the knock to the head and the event just witnessed.

He removed the magazine from the rifle with an angry glare. He shook his head to remove the spite from his mind. It was never the gun. It was who was shooting it.

A stare up the incline meant a long careful climb ahead. With the aches throbbing through his muscles, he inhaled deeply and began his way up the incline. A second thought reminded him how he got this far down the slope.

The only female who could let out that shrill cry was the one he had brought with him.

CHAPTER SIXTEEN

Cole ran to the top of a clearing. Looking into the valley, he tried to spot the path. The dense forest hid all from view. He threaded his way through the trees with the Mouton in both hands, at the ready should trouble come his way.

Using bullet holes in the trees as landmarks, he was able to guide himself to where Omaha Sam lay. From there he was able to find the spot where he found Charlie's body. He scanned right. The path could barely be seen in the dimming light.

He approached slowly through the trees, looking for the China girl. He crept silently, his fingers around the trigger. As he neared the position, he didn't see the girl or the palomino. A quick count in his mind named all that he came with on the ferry. With the foreigner fellow gone, perhaps there lay another assassin in wait.

Not wanting to become an easy target, he went to the bend in the path for a better angle to see into the trees. Once there, he saw three men. Two held rifles.

The one holding the girl by the arm appeared familiar, but he couldn't remember from where. By the looks of their clothes, they weren't men accustomed to travel. More like workers, maybe even miners by the smears on their faces. Either way, he was sure they could shoot a gun and therefore didn't want to make it easy for them.

He crept back up an incline. An overhang gave him a better vantage point to see all three men and the girl. He could take all three with the Mouton, but that might get the girl killed.

"You there," he yelled. All of them looked about trying to sight him, but none seemed to be able to. "What's your business?"

The one with the girl shouted back. "Why don't you come down here and find out for yourself."

It seemed he'd heard the voice before, too. "No. I can see you fine right where I'm at. Who you be?"

The one with the girl grinned. The split tooth smile was as good as the name. "You mean you don't remember me? That kind of hurts my feelings." He put his hand around the girl's throat. "Kind of gets me in a bad mood. If you were to come down and talk awhile, maybe it'd put me back in a better frame of mind."

The action put the Mouton to aim. Despite the gun's accuracy, the distance made it a risky shot to not hit the girl. As he pondered his choices, the other two with the rifles seemed to be more appealing targets. As he took aim, he considered what he was about to cause. All of this, him being in this forest, was at the whim of other people. He made another choice.

"Will? Will Hayward, that's your name, ain't it?"

When he saw the split-tooth smile, he knew he had their attention. "Listen here. All you men need to go back to your jobs and leave the girl be."

The warning only made them laugh. It appeared they'd only understand a simpler message. Cole took careful aim. The shots needed to be precisely placed. Once in his sights, he squeezed the trigger. The Mouton roared.

The shot sent a large hole through the tree. The hole was easily noticed over the shoulder of the first rifleman. Cole pumped the action and quickly sent another slug into the tree nearest the second.

Both men crouched, scanning about to see where the shots came from. Even Will seemed spooked by the sudden blasts. As the two bobbed their heads left and right, one more shot was needed to convince them. The boom echoed through the forest, sending dirt and leaves up into the air at their feet. It did the trick. The two of them dropped their rifles and ran down the path.

Cole concentrated on Will, who didn't seem swayed. Will drew a knife and put it against the girl's throat.

"I'll cut her throat. Come out and show yourself or she's dead."

Cole lowered the Mouton. It wasn't so much his fear of hitting the girl. He'd made tougher shots. A gnawing at his gut got him on his feet and down the slope. Slowly, he walked through the forest and came to the edge of the path. "Let her go," he said, emerging into the sunlight with the rifle raised at his shoulder.

Will increased his grip of the girl's chin, twisting the knife in his hand like he was about to give a shave. "Drop the rifle or I'll cut her open. I swear."

Cole kept walking straight for them. He peeked at the girl's wide, panicked eyes. He spoke in a calm tone to keep her and Will from moving. "Hear me. There are five men dead in these woods. Hired killers that knew the risk. It don't require much reckoning to figure how they got that way." As he crossed the path, he steadied the rifle. Despite Will's intensified grasp on the girl, Cole didn't slow.

"Put down the rifle. Then we'll have ourselves a real fight. We'll finish what we started." Cole was in no mood. Still at a steady march, he angled the barrel up. "I said put down the rifle. I'll slice her like a pig." Will pressed the blade against the girl's throat.

Cole didn't stop. He pressed the barrel against Will's forehead. "If you cut her, what do you think I'll do to you? Listen hard. I've done enough killing for today. Now your friends have gone. You tell them any tale you like. About how you bested me with a knife. Made me squeal for my own life. Won't have no shame for it. But the one thing I ain't going to let you do is hurt the girl. She's got no part in this." Cole darted his eyes at her, then at him. "So, Will, put down your knife, turn her loose, give yourself some time and then join your friends. Go back to your mine. Have a snort or two. Find a woman if you ain't got one. Do this, and I'll let you live."

Will's eyes peeked up at the barrel. He inhaled heavily, his eyes constantly peeking up, then at Cole. In a gradual motion, he lowered the knife from the girl's throat, and soon after let his grasp sag from her chin. She jumped away from him.

Cole eased the barrel away from Will's forehead. The miner's shoulders slumped as he walked to the path. Cole watched him all the way, until Will was safely out of sight. The China girl came to him and wrapped her arms around his chest.

CHAPTER SEVENTEEN

Cole kept his back turned as the ferry approached. He motioned for the girl to stay hidden in the brush. He hoped the foreigner's coat would provide the needed cover to keep the ship on its course. As it neared, he checked his load. Once confident for the third time in an hour the cylinder was full, he snapped shut the chambergate and waited.

The rhythmic clack of the steam engine signaled the ship was about on shore. He needed to hear a familiar voice. Soon, he heard just that. "I trust you had good hunting." Chester's voice was the welcome needed to spring the trap. Cole faced around with the Colt outstretched, aimed and cocked.

"Matter of fact I did."

Chester's grin shrank in an instant. "What are you doing here?"

"Surprised?" The answer to Cole's question was written on Chester's face. Cole pointed the pistol at the captain. "Try to turn this boat and I'll drop you into the water." Cole put the aim back on Chester. "I'll have your piece. Throw it on the deck." A few moments passed before the weapon was reluctantly surrendered. Cole motioned for the ramp to be lowered and the single crewman complied. He waved and the China girl came running from the high weeds. They both boarded the ferry. Cole kept the aim steady on Chester as he picked the piece off the deck and tucked it in his belt. "Met the fellow that owned this coat. Maybe you know him? Some foreigner with a real mean smile."

Chester looked to the coat, then at Cole. "Did you kill him?"

Cole shook his head. Spite flowed through his veins. "No. No, that job was left to nature. I can't say for sure how, but something close to the hand of the Almighty swept him right off a cliff. Amazing thing to see."

Chester seemed confused at the reference. His eyes drifted to the girl in logger's clothes. "You brought one with you? Did you take to a piece of her?"

The reference got Cole's goat. "About as often as you take to this." He whipped the Colt across Chester's head, dropping the man in a heap on the floor. The crewman took a step toward Cole. With the Colt turned on the young man the approach was stopped. "Got no feud with you, son. Just do as I say and you'll walk off the boat with all your parts in place."

As the ferry continued through the bay, Cole ran thoughts through his head. Nothing seemed clear. All he knew was there wouldn't be peace for him until he addressed the source of the problem.

About the time he could see the buildings of the city, the captain's call came, and at the same time

Chester woke from the blow. Cole snatched the collar of the bleeding man. "We're going to go see your boss."

The ferry came to port. Cole waved the Colt at the captain and the crewman to get into one of the holds. Once they were under lock and key, he motioned for the girl to follow him off the boat. "Make a sound and it'll be your last," he warned Chester.

He had to be discreet with the pistol at Chester's back. Should someone notice, he might draw the attention of one of those shotgun toters. He did see some eyes cast his way, but they appeared more concerned with the China girl. Before they made their way up the street, a red building caught Cole's eye and spawned a thought. "Wait." He pushed Chester to the building. Soon they were at the Albatross sign. "Open the door." Chester slowly complied with the order. Cole shoved him inside.

The darkness of the bar took time for his vision to adjust. He didn't want to stay too long and answer many questions. "Is O'Bannion here?"

"What do you want?" came the answer from the dim interior.

"This man is kidnapping me," Chester yelled. In reaction, Cole whipped the pistol against the back of Chester's head, but not with the same force as before. He scanned the dark. Not a soul moved to rescue the dapper man.

"What do you want in here?" O'Bannion's loud yell reminded Cole why he'd come.

"It's me. Cole." He took the China girl by the arm. "I want you to take this girl and find a safe place for her." She looked back at him with eyes wide. He didn't have time to calm to her fears. He had to trust she would understand. By her long face, the idea wasn't off to a good start.

The barkeep shook his head. "I ain't no caretaker of women. Especially Chinese."

Cole didn't have time to plead the point. He focused his eyes on O'Bannion, so he didn't have to look into the girl's eyes. He pushed her further toward the bar. "Just take her. Find a place where she'll be safe. You know better than me. See to her and I'll see that you'll get paid for it." He snatched Chester's collar once more and lifted the man to his feet. When they turned for the door, another question came from the bar.

"Where are you going?"

"To settle another debt." He opened the door without looking at her and pushed Chester outside. The dapper man was groggy from the blow, or so he acted. Cole wasn't concerned with the man's health. He shoved him to walk to the corner.

"What do you think you're going to do? March up into The Palace? Demand to see Ambrose Waterfield at gunpoint?"

"Could be just the way it's going to happen." They rounded the corner. A trolley began its journey up the steep street. The idea of riding up the hill rather than walk it was an easier solution and would attract less eyes. He shoved Chester to the train car. Controlling him by the collar like reins on a horse, he waited until the trolley was in motion. Then he pushed Chester and they grabbed onto the iron landing. "Remember what I told you. One word and I'll put a bullet in your back."

Cole scanned about for any curious eyes, especially any belonging to those shotgun-toting vigilantes. With a firm grip on Chester's coat, he kept

his eyes peeled for any movement, and his right
hand poking the Colt's muzzle in Chester's back
gave him the threat needed to keep the man quiet.

The steep angle forced him back against the rail.
Chester flinched an elbow, partly to catch his balance and partly to test Cole. The hammer went back
on the pistol. "One more time and I'll dump your
body in the street." The sure promise of death was
enough to keep the dapper man from further attempts to escape or seek help.

After leveling onto three cross streets, then returning to the steep angle, the trolley slowed as it
came by The Palace. Before it came to a complete
stop where others would leave the train car, Cole
snatched Chester's collar and steered the man up
the step.

Looking at the front, better sense came to mind.
Should they march in, Chester would be surrounded not only by friends, but likely by some on
his payroll. "Wait," he said. Chester took an extra
step, but Cole yanked him back. "Not that way."

"If you leave now," Chester said, "you can get
out of the city with your life."

Cole shoved him toward the corner. "So you can
send more of your gunnies on my trail? I think I'll
stay a while longer. I may take your life if you don't
hush your mouth." They rounded the corner. With
less attention from others on the side street, Cole
marched Chester to a side entrance. They walked
through the garden to a door with a glass pane in
the center. When they entered the building, Chester
removed his hat for an unescorted lady. When he
bowed slightly, she saw the pistol.

With the fury of a storm gale, she screamed, lifting
the hem of her skirt off the ground and scampering

down the hall. Certain she would bring more unwanted attention, Cole grabbed Chester by the nape and forced him down the hall toward the lobby. At a quick pace they neared the stairway. A tunic-dressed servant froze in his steps at their approach.

"Ambrose Waterfield in there?" Cole asked as they passed.

"No," was the answer. Cole yanked on Chester's hair the same as a mane on a mustang, stopping him in an instant. "Mr. Waterfield has retired to his room."

"Where's that?" Cole yelled. The servant saw the pistol, then receded against the wall with eyes wide. Cole didn't have time or patience to ask again. He pointed the Colt at the servant. "Where!"

"Second floor. Room two-oh-one."

As soon as the words were said, Cole rammed Chester down the hall and to the stairs. More screams from behind hastened his step. Voices from the lobby stirred his attention.

"Have you met Vivien Hooper yet? She's here, you know."

The mention broke his concentration. Two women strolled to the stairs. However, when the speaker saw Cole, they both changed their path and scurried back to the main lobby. Cole couldn't stop to ask more questions. With more folks aware of his handling of Chester, he knew it wouldn't be long before the local law arrived. He pushed Chester up the stairs. The usual smug grin wasn't there, but the confidence still stood present as they went to the second floor. Unsure if he'd be gunned down, Cole knew he had to finish what he started.

He shoved Chester down the hall. The first room

on the right had the numbers 201 on the door. Cole stopped and tapped the door with the Colt. "Tell him you're here."

"Tell him yourself," Chester sniped. "They'll come for you, you know. You can't get out of here."

The notion occurred to Cole as well. With no answer and feeling mite naked in the hall, he lifted his boot. "Might as well get this over with." He rammed his heel at the latch and busted open the door. He shoved Chester inside. Once he entered the room, Waterfield stood in shock, slowly removing the cigar from his mouth.

"What is this? What is going on?"

Cole glanced at him as he shut the door and propped a chair against the broken latch. "Ain't happy to see me?"

Waterfield looked to Chester. "Why is this man here?"

While rising to his knees, Chester rubbed the back of his neck. "He killed Koenig. And Charlie Biggersby and the others. He's here to do us harm." The remark boiled Cole's blood.

"Do you harm? Is that what you call it when you kill people?"

"Kill people?" Waterfield questioned with surprise. "What do you mean 'kill people'?"

Cole pointed the Colt at him. "You sent us— Charlie, Bits, Monroe, Sam, Tom Perkins, all of us— to murder Chinese. To run them off the land, so to sell it for timber."

The elder man curled his brow in a puzzled manner. "Chinese? What are you saying?" He looked to Chester. "Is what he's saying true?"

Now Chester appeared confused as he sat on the floor. "He's figured it out."

"Figured what out?" Waterfield's lack of knowledge seemed convincing. Cole wasn't sure if it was an act.

"You wanted us to kill those people. Killers from different parts, not known to nobody. Drifters. So it'd look like we were bandits. Just out to rob and murder. The talk would be that it was all lawlessness by a bunch of strangers. And once we were done," he said with a nod to the both of them, "then, you'd have to make sure we didn't talk." He shrugged. "Who would miss us?"

Waterfield darted his view to Cole, then to Chester. Finally, he shook his head. "I don't know anything about this. If any of this is true, it was misguided by him," he said, pointing at Chester. "I can't be held accountable."

"What!" Chester's angered shout drew Cole's attention. The dapper man's brow furrowed, narrowing his eyes. "What are you trying? To blame me for all this?"

Waterfield looked at Cole. "You see? He's shifting responsibility to me. You must believe me. I am a prominent businessman. I only knew about some vagrants that he had told me about. That is why I offered you the job to remove them. I had no idea about murder."

"Stop it, stop it," Chester interrupted. "Stop the lies."

Waterfield pointed at him, still looking at the bewildered Cole. "This man is delirious. He doesn't know what he's talking about. You must believe me. He can't be trusted. I've always suspected him of being disloyal."

"You ungrateful bastard," Chester growled. "After all I've done for you." He reached for Cole's belt.

Before Cole could move the Colt, Chester had grabbed the piece tucked in the belt. As quick as a blink, he pointed and fired at Waterfield. The shot sent a hole through the center of his chest. Blood spewing from the white shirt meant the slug pierced the heart. Waterfield fell backward, crashing onto his chair and spilling onto the floor.

Cole turned the Colt at Chester. Voices and shrieks came through the door. The chair propped under the latch wouldn't hold very long. Cole, still surprised by the shooting, didn't know whether to fire or lower the Colt. An instant's thought convinced him to leave.

Chester appeared in a daze. With glassy eyes, he peered up at Cole, the piece still pointed in Waterfield's direction and smoking from the muzzle. As the shouts in the hall rose, Cole looked to the window. Every second brought more thoughts of blame coming his way. He looked to the body. Blood now dripped from the distinguished beard.

The chair against the door creaked from the pressure. Cole again looked to the window. With Chester still in a daze, Cole opened the window and peered down. The distance wasn't the longest he'd jumped, but he'd rather seek another escape. The landing led to an iron staircase leading further up the side of the building. Certain he'd find another window to open, he stepped out onto the landing. As he took the first step of the climb, another gunshot boomed from the window.

CHAPTER EIGHTEEN

He stared at the dark blue sky hovering over the sea while he stood in the bright sunlight. Normally he counted on a storm. However, the last two weeks taught him not to expect what he knew. The notion made him peek at his own clothes. Not his own choice, but he felt he needed to get done what his gut told him he had to do. It was what he'd come all this way for.

He walked up the steps to The Palace. The last time he left the place, he walked among glares; now, he was hardly noticed as he strode inside. The rumor held she was somewhere in the building, but he couldn't go to every door. It would take another two weeks.

The faces of the rest of the people swarming about the lobby didn't remind him of her. He looked about in the halls near those rising rooms and around the stairs. He didn't see her. Next, he thought to check the dining hall, which was full of folks having their breakfast. He'd tested himself in the worst of gun battles during his short time in

California, but that didn't give him enough courage to stroll among the tables in case he came across her. He searched from the door, but still didn't spot her red hair.

After near an hour of lurking about for her, he finally sucked up enough gumption to go to the counter where the keys were kept. He looked the young clerk in the eye, grunting his throat clear. He didn't want to say the name too loud. He opened his mouth, but another voice with the same words stopped his tongue.

"Miss Vivien Hooper! Message for Miss Vivien Hooper!" one of the tunic-dressed servants shouted among the clutch of folks in the lobby. Cole waved away at the clerk in an act of dismissing his need, then cautiously followed the servant from a safe distance. As the call continued, a watchful eye was kept for any presence of her. While Cole kept a lookout for any woman with red hair who might respond, a man with slick dark hair with gray on the side came forward and signaled the servant. This fellow stood short and slim in stature. He, like those around him, wore a dark dress coat with a shiny silver vest over a stiff-collared white shirt and wide dark tie with a stick pin stuck in the middle. A thin mustache sprinkled with gray was trimmed in a tight line above the top lip.

The fellow took the envelope from the servant and put a coin in the white-gloved hand. Why this fellow took a note meant for Vivien Hooper angered Cole. It appeared an act of thievery. His blood pumping a bit faster, he was approaching the man when a flash of red to the right caught his eye. It stopped him like a wall.

He watched her, the hair pinned under a small

hat, a dark blue dress angling her shape down to the slim waist, over the petite hips all the way to the floor. His breath stopped. His heart pounded.

Needing to steady his nerve, he inhaled deeply. His approach to the man he thought was stealing the note brought him too close to hide. As she spoke a few words to the fellow, Cole's legs became stuck, as if nailed to the floor just a few feet away from her. In a few seconds he couldn't help but be seen. At first, she peeked at him, continued her talk, then gave him a full look. He couldn't keep his eyes off her, still in awe of finally finding who he sought.

She showed her polite but sly smile. "Hello. Can I help you?"

He didn't recognize the voice. It didn't have the same cut. Caught in the moment, he shook himself free from his trance. "No," he replied. The fool's answer made him say the first words on his tongue. "I thought you were somebody I know."

She appeared surprised and pleased. "Really?" she responded with a giggle. She shot a look at the fellow with the envelope, then looked back at Cole. "Well, I am so sorry. I don't recall having made your acquaintance." She raised her hand in a style consistent with a woman of manners. He took it inside his with little spirit. "My name is Vivien Hooper."

Sure of her name, he didn't want to brag about it. It wouldn't be proper to remind her of their last meeting in her dressing room in the theater. Not in front of this fellow. Still, her lack of a familiar response to him slowed his beating heart. Maybe it was the clothes. The last time he wore his usually dusty duds and almost a month's worth of whiskers. When he recalled how she had shaved them off, he remembered that the light in the room wasn't all that bright. It might have been too dark for her to get a good look at him. His spirit restored, he couldn't resist a smile. "Clay. Clay Cole."

"Mr. Cole, so nice to meet you."

Her reply didn't help him maintain that spirit. She should have known his name. She released his hand and turned to the fellow with the envelope.

"May I introduce my husband? James Earnest Moore. Darling, this is Mr. Clay Cole."

Cole couldn't move. For an instant, not a muscle, including the one pushing his lungs, would move. He must have heard her wrong. She didn't say her last name with his. It must not be what his ears told him. The instant passed. The fellow extended his hand. There was nothing left to do but be friendly. Cole forced a smile and shook the man's hand, bewilderment twisting his thoughts.

"You're her husband?"

Moore looked to Vivien. "Why, yes. For seven glorious years."

He held the man's hand for an instant longer, running through his mind all that happened to him the last seven years. He was in Montana, strapped to a tree next to the Little Bighorn River watching Custer lead five companies of men to their death. The event caused a wince to this day every time someone mentioned his own name. It stood as the worst day in his life. Now, he imagined that about the same time this beautiful woman was marrying this man whose hand he now held. So many thoughts ran through his mind, he couldn't stop one long enough to speak it, except one.

"That makes you a real lucky fellow." He couldn't help get the peculiarity out of his head. "How is it her name ain't your'n?"

It took a brief instant for the man to understand, then reply. "Oh, well, Vivien is a stage actress and an entertainer. She is known widely by her maiden name. It is very common among women in the business."

"Yes," she added, sliding her arm under and over his. "Besides being my husband, James is also my manager and agent."

Cole didn't understand. "Is that like your boss?"

Although he found no humor to it, the couple chuckled at the remark. "In a way, yes," she answered. "He tells me what to do. And I follow his advice completely." She finished by giving Moore a peck on the cheek.

Cole had no call to feel that way, but just the same, his chest felt as if a blade had just been plunged through it. A breath was needed to pull his lungs out of his throat. In that moment, he realized that all he had to come to believe was just a dream he'd had back in that cell in Copper Springs, Montana. He never really saw her dance and sing from backstage. Nor did he follow her up to her dressing room, share a drink of fancy liquor, share the same tub, feel her soft skin against his callused flesh, or share any of the primal sensations of nature between a man and woman. It was a cruel trick his mind had played. There was nobody to blame. Especially this well-mannered fellow, or the red-haired lady hanging on his arm.

Cole shook his head. "Well, I'm sorry for taking up your time."

"What is the name of the person you thought was me?" she asked.

Not sure how to answer, he let his memory of that dream speak for him. "It was a woman said her given name was Vivien Hoogenpuhl. She was from a place I can't hardly say right. Auster, Austra-lia."

"Australia?" Her eyes opened. "Oh my, no. I'm not from there. I am from Burnham, Pennsylvania, just outside of Philadelphia." She gazed at her husband. "We've never even been there."

Cole shook his head to dismiss his foolish words. "Pay no mind. It ain't something for you to fret over." About to turn around, his last words were interrupted by Moore.

"That reminds me, dear," he said to her. "I've just received word that Mrs. Livingston has been struck ill with fever. She won't be meeting us in Seattle."

Her eyes opened wide. "Oh goodness, no. I hope she is going to be all right." She paused in thought, her mouth still ajar. "That means I won't have an attendant for the performance. Where on Earth would I get one at this late date?"

Cole's mind snapped back into the present. "That like a helper?"

Vivien looked at him with her big eyes, the ones only women possessed when they needed a problem solved and would be beholden to whomever solved it. The solution was right in the front of his brain. "I know a woman. A girl really. She's real good at helping. Wouldn't need much for pay. Room and board might be all she's needing."

The offer appeared to interest both of them. "Just how old a girl is this?" asked Moore.

Cole thought about when he first saw the China girl. "I'd say twenty."

"That sounds very young," Vivien said with concern.

"Oh, for a white girl that might be true." When both of their brows shot up like fresh-lit candles,

Cole knew he needed to explain. "See, she's Chinese. But not from here in the city. She's a real worker." He remembered another delusion he'd had with the red-haired beauty on his mind. "She's real good at tending to the needs of others. Kind of how she was brought up, to think of them first."

"Well, then where is she?" Moore asked with renewed interest.

Cole wondered exactly how he would be able to retrieve the girl. "Tell you what, I'll get her for you." He took a step toward the door. "Should take about an hour."

Vivien's brow again shot up as she looked to her husband. "Is that enough time?"

Moore pulled a watch from his pocket. "Our ship leaves in ninety minutes," he said staring at the watch. Then he looked at Cole. "Are you sure you can make it in an hour?"

Cole returned the look, then his eyes drifted to Vivien. "Yeah," he said with a nod. "I'll make it." He turned for the door with her face still alighted in his memory. Past the front doors, he made his way down the incline as he had his first night in San Francisco. As if in a trance, he thought about all that he'd come for and how he was now doing a favor that would take her away from him.

When he made the turn on the wharf, he sighted the now-familiar red brick building. He came to the twin doors with the bird above flapping in the mild breeze. He went inside and found himself wrapped by the gloomy interior. Many a patron huddled about the bar, but he shouldered his way to the front. Only his size persuaded them to spread enough to get an elbow on the bar.

With a towel on his shoulder, O'Bannion came to

the end. About halfway, he stopped and opened his eyes wide. "Is that my old pal, Clay Cole?" Cole nodded, not wanting to bring too much attention, but the now-friendly barkeep came at him with a smile and hand held out for all to notice. "Why are you in those clothes this time? I thought you were a cowpoke. Don't tell me those Nob Hill bastards have changed you again."

"No," Cole answered with a shake of the head. "It's all I have to wear at the time." Before another question could be asked, the barkeep went to the end to serve his customers.

"Where is the girl?" Cole asked, then repeated in a louder voice. Neither attempt was heard and paid attention to until he yelled. "Where's Lulu?" The shout was enough to get attention. Once the barkeep took payment for the liquor served, he returned to Cole's end of the bar.

"Why do you want her?"

"I think I may have found a place for her." Cole stated the reply with some pride. However, it appeared not what O'Bannion wanted to hear. The barkeep poured a few more drinks. The act seemed one not encouraged by the news. Cole leaned closer on the crowded bar. "So, where is she?"

It took a moment before the barkeep finished wiping his hands on the towel. Finally, he turned to Cole. "What if I found a place for her?"

The spirited wind left Cole's body. "What did you do with her?"

Like a child caught in a lie, O'Bannion shrugged at Cole. "Well, I couldn't very well keep her around here. She'd scared off my customers. Orientals aren't exactly welcome on the wharf. She's better off with her own. They have their own part of the city."

Cole let his head dip to the wood. "Where did you send her?"

"She's probably gone. Those people don't exactly care about their own, neither. She's likely been sold."

Cole's head shot up. "Is that what you did? You sold her?"

The barkeep went to the far end of the bar and proceeded to wipe glasses. Cole didn't have the time or patience to play waiting games. He stepped back from the bar and went around the mass to get to the end. Once able to pry his way through the throng, he faced O'Bannion again. "You sold her, didn't you? Made some money for yourself."

"You said to make sure she was in a safe place. No safer place than with her own people. Why shouldn't I make a commission on the transaction?" O'Bannion ladled soup into two bowls.

Cole waved his head about. "You can't sell people no more. Slavery is against the law now. Did you not hear about the war among the states?"

"I didn't sell no slave," the barkeep sniped. "I found the girl a place to stay in the city and they paid me for my service." He took the bowls to the far end of the bar where Cole first stood.

Now, time crept into Cole's mind. If he was to find the girl at all, much less in the time before Vivien Hooper left on a ship, he had to get the respect needed to find the answers. He might have been wearing the duds of a fancy dude, but he still carried the means needed for life on the prairie. He reached in his coat and drew the Colt pistol from his belt. In a confident manner, he thumbed the hammer back and fired into the floor.

The shot brought all eyes and ears his way, but

not one voice spoke except his. "How do I find her?"

With smoke still drifting around the lamps, the barkeep looked at him with wide eyes. "She's in Chinatown."

Cole's tone reflected his surly mood. "That's where she is. I said how do I find her. I ain't going to knock on every door in the place."

O'Bannion looked to the door, then to the shadows at the near end of the bar. Cole knew who usually stood there. He pointed the Colt to the shadows. "I know you're in there. I don't have time to trade punches with you." He turned the pistol at O'Bannion. "How do I find her?"

The barkeep shifted his eyes to the door and pointed. "You go out here and steer left. If the breeze is at your back you'll pick up the smell of noodles a-cooking with a strong scent of salt. Then when you've got the scent—"

Cole fired another round into the floor. "Enough of your babbling."

"I took her to a Chinaman goes by the name of Canton Eddie."

"Is that a pimp?" When Cole didn't get an answer, he cocked the hammer once more.

"Hold your fire, damn you, Clay Cole. The rats have enough holes to crawl into here as it is." He nodded his head. "Yes, he's a pimp in Chinatown."

With the hope the story stood some truth, Cole felt the time drip away. Since he only knew a handful of places in the city, he turned the gun to the shadows. "You're going to show me the way." In a moment, the hulking mass of Little John came into the dim light of the bar. The giant first looked to O'Bannion, who then nodded as a sign of compliance.

Little John peeked at Cole, only to pass by and head for the door. Cole scanned about for any guns that could be pointed at his back. Once he had backed out of the door, he looked the giant in the eye. Little John appeared ready to show the way.

They both walked up the never-easing incline. Cole watched the shops on the sidewalk, which were full of people. No one seemed even interested as he and the giant walked by. With the turn of a corner the entire face of the city changed. It became the face of a different land. Although there were plenty of people on the street, not one was white.

Unlike the corner before, Cole couldn't help notice all eyes on him and Little John as they proceeded down another street. Words were shouted at them that didn't sound like those of welcome. Unsure at first, he soon realized that many times whites must have raided these streets in an effort to rid the city of their kind. He tried to ignore their insults. Even though not understanding a single word, the message was an easy one to comprehend. It wasn't the first time he'd been in a foreign land on his own soil where the locals were of another culture.

Little John abruptly stopped and pointed up a rickety staircase on the side of the building.

"That's where she is?" Little John just nodded. About to go up, a nagging sense stopped him. He looked into the giant's eyes. "You ever say anything?"

Little John shook his head and uttered noises and sounds, but no audible words. In that moment, he understood why the giant worked at the Albatross.

It was the only job where his size did all the talking for him.

"You wait here," Cole ordered, pointing at the sidewalk. He went up the stairs carefully, not only to be sure of the worn, weathered boards, but also in case the landlord wasn't in a friendly mood. He came to the top landing. To knock on the door probably wouldn't get him what he wanted. He pulled the Colt and opened the chambergate to count the fresh shells. With two gone, he'd might need the remaining four. He flipped the gate shut with his thumb, took a deep breath and kicked in the door.

Two whores rose off the floor and ran. Their customer stayed on the floor with the opium pipe still stuck in his mouth. Cole followed the whores through a beaded curtain. He went to the first door as they ran further down the hall. He opened the door. A fat Chinaman lay atop a thinner China whore. Once certain it wasn't her, he closed the door from the repulsive sight.

The next door to the right was stuck. The flimsy door would likely tear like paper with a kick. He tucked the Colt in his belt and rammed his shoulder against it twice. When the jamb shattered, Cole stumbled into the room. Another older Chinaman continued his business undisturbed. Cole went to the side of the cot-like bed. There she was.

"Get off her," he yelled. When the Chinaman didn't even slow his pace, Cole grabbed a handful of hair and wrenched the man off the cot. Jabbered words were hurled at him, but Cole looked to the girl. Tears filled her eyes. He held out his hand and pulled her to her feet. She pulled the thin dress down over her hips to its normal form.

The customer, now realizing his ride was over

went to his pants on the chair. From the belt he drew a butcher knife as a threat. Cole pulled the revolver from his own belt. The sign of the seven-inch barrel at the bridge of his nose was enough for the customer to yield the path to the door.

Cole wasted no time proceeding out of the room, through the hall and toward the door. With the girl's hand in his, he went through the front room, but loud jabbering from a different voice came from where the first two whores had gone. A double-barreled shotgun came from an older Chinaman. Before he was going to trade lead in such a small place, Cole thought of another solution. "Canton Eddie. That you?"

The Chinaman stopped, but didn't lower the shotgun. "Yeah, yeah, yeah," was the answer, each with a bob of the head. "You steal. You steal."

Cole looked to the girl. While still holding the Colt on the man, he carefully put his hand in his pocket and pulled out a roll of money. He tossed it Canton Eddie. "Bought and paid." Without any more bargaining, he pushed the girl out of the door and they both stepped quickly down the staircase. Cole nodded at Little John to lead the way.

After two corners, he realized the garment the girl had on wasn't one to meet Vivien Hooper. He scanned about and found a red dress with gold patterns respective of the culture. It looked slim enough, so he took it off the rack. The shop owner came out with a hand extended. Cole pointed back at the rickety stairs. "Canton Eddie. He has the money."

Not sure if he was understood, or if the shop owner was frightened by the mention of the local pimp, or maybe he glimpsed the Colt still in Cole's hand, he rushed back into the shop.

Cole took the girl by the hand. He glanced at the sun. Having gauged it all his life, he knew time had slipped away faster than he thought. They had to get back to the wharf.

At a trot, they wound through the streets, still with some calls from the angry locals in their unknown language, but Cole didn't stop. If they did, there might be some local law officers of the Chinese, and he didn't want to have a gun battle on their streets. Little John soon charged in front. With his mass leading them, it was like a plow through soil and they ran through the furrow.

When they left Chinatown, Cole took a sigh of relief. They passed by two streets and soon the surroundings became familiar even for him. They came upon the red brick building. Little John stopped like an engine out of fuel. Cole couldn't stop just to thank him. A wave had to suffice.

They came around a bend and the shape of a line took form. The more they ran, the straighter the line. An instant later, Cole saw the sidewheel of the ship. This had to be the one. He glanced back to point it out to the girl, but she still had on the skintight shimmy. Cole stopped her and took a few steps to an alley. Once there, he made sure no drunks lived there, then motioned for her to change. She nodded, but his frantic waving only served to panic her face.

It wasn't long before he understood she needed privacy. "Hurry," he gritted. He left the alley and stood guard from any prying eyes. While he waited, he spotted the red-haired beauty. She and Moore stood just feet away from the gangway. Cole strayed from the alley in order to get their attention. He waved. They saw him. As they came toward him, he walked to them.

"We thought you wouldn't make it," said Vivien. There was something in her eyes which sent his heart pounding. It was the look of faith. "But I see you have delivered."

In an instant, Cole's heart stopped. She'd left the alley. When he turned, his eyes caught sight of the red color. About to sidestep what he first saw, his brain recognized not only the Chinese dress, but the Chinese girl wearing it. She looked beautiful.

Cole faced about once more. "Here she is," he said, taking the girl by the arm, reminding himself to be gentle. Vivien's eyes lit up. Moore gave Cole a pleased smile. Cole stood by her side, not sure what to do next. Vivien held out her hand for the girl. "Hello. My name is Vivien Hooper. What is yours?"

The girl didn't answer. She looked to Cole. He knew the expression. "Her name is Lulu."

"Doesn't she speak English?" asked Moore.

"Well," Cole started trying to think of an answer. All the time he'd spent with the girl came to mind. "All you need do is point. She understands more than you think. I bet if you were to talk to her while you're pointing, she'll reckon what you're talking about."

Vivien appeared amused. "She looks like she'll do just fine."

Moore drew the watch from his pocket. "We'll need to get aboard." Vivien held out her hand for the girl to take. Luan stood firm.

She peeked at Cole. He waved for her to go forward. "Go on." She took only a single step. He waved at her again. "Get." Luan turned and faced

Vivien. They joined hands and took to each other like two peas in a pod.

Moore extended his hand. "I'm not sure this is going to work itself out, but I thank you for your help, sir."

Cole shook Moore's hand, but he kept looking at the women as they started up the gangway. Vivien faced about and looked at Cole while her husband went to her side. "You do now look familiar to me, Mr. Cole. Perhaps we have met before."

"My dear, we need to leave," Moore said with a firm tone.

Vivien stood her ground. "I remember seeing a man in Montana. He was in a jail. They called him something." Her eyes lit up. "Rainmaker."

Although his heart pounded at her mention, it was not a time to share what he was feeling. Not a time to tell her all that he'd come through just to meet her. It was not his time at all. He shook his head. "No. That weren't me."

Her husband took her hand and led her up the gangway. Luan was close by her side. When they got to the top, Vivien turned around, her face filled with awe as she stared at him. He knew she realized the truth, but it wasn't his place to use it to any advantage.

Once more, she was turned by the arm of her husband. The China girl also stayed a moment longer at the rail. Moore's voice beckoned her away from view as the crew threw the gangway on the wharf. The sidewheel churned the water, making its way away from the dock.

He stood watching the ship as it went farther into the bay. Once he convinced himself there was no reason for it to come back, he faced about and looked upon the city. San Francisco was all that was talked about. However, it wasn't a place for him to stay. Too many customs for him to get along with made for a bad mix. He resisted a final look into the bay and started up the damn incline once more. Arizona was a far-off place.

MANHUNT
Tim McGuire

Living as a wanted man for the past six years has been mighty tough for Clay Cole. The man known far and wide as the Rainmaker has been running from the law for a crime he didn't commit. Now Clay's stopped running. The Rainmaker is determined to clear his name once and for all. But the law has something far more dangerous in mind for Clay. A brutal killer has escaped from prison with the aid of his gang and a Gatling gun—and he's taken Clay's friend as a hostage. The sheriff knows the Rainmaker is the perfect man to track down a killer. And Clay will do anything to rescue his friend…even if it's the last thing he does as a free man.

MAX BRAND

PETER BLUE

Peter Blue was one of the most feared gunmen in the West. But now he's holed up in a small shack, hiding from the world. For he doesn't want anyone to know about the bullet that's destroyed his right hand, his gun hand. He realizes it won't be long before he's found and another man comes to challenge him. After all, he's made plenty of enemies in his lifetime. But he's determined to be ready for them—with the fastest left-handed draw they've ever seen. If only he can get his fingers to stop trembling and his aim to hold true...